SPECIAL MESSAGE

THE ULVERSCROFT FOUNDATION
(registered UK charity number 264873)
was established in 1972 to provide funds for research, diagnosis and treatment of eye diseases.
Examples of major projects funded by the Ulverscroft Foundation are:-

- The Children's Eye Unit at Moorfields Eye Hospital, London
- The Ulverscroft Children's Eye Unit at Great Ormond Street Hospital for Sick Children
- Funding research into eye diseases and treatment at the Department of Ophthalmology, University of Leicester
- The Ulverscroft Vision Research Group, Institute of Child Health
- Twin operating theatres at the Western Ophthalmic Hospital, London
- The Chair of Ophthalmology at the Royal Australian College of Ophthalmologists

You can help further the work of the Foundation by making a donation or leaving a legacy.
Every contribution is gratefully received. If you would like to help support the Foundation or require further information, please contact:

THE ULVERSCROFT FOUNDATION
The Green, Bradgate Road, Anstey
Leicester LE7 7FU, England
Tel: (0116) 236 4325

website: www.foundation.ulverscroft.com

Jeffrey Archer has topped the bestseller lists around the world, with sales of over 275 million copies. He is the only author ever to have been a number-one bestseller in fiction (nineteen times), short stories (four times), and non-fiction (*The Prison Diaries*). He is married with two sons and lives in London and Cambridge.

You can find out more about the author at www.jeffreyarcher.co.uk

TELL TALE

This new collection of short stories offers an insight into the people Jeffrey Archer has met, the tales he has heard, and the countries he has visited during the past ten years. Find out what happens to the hapless young detective from Naples who travels to an Italian hillside town to find out *Who Killed the Mayor?* and the pretentious schoolboy in *The Road to Damascus* whose discovery of the origins of his father's wealth changes his life in the most profound way. Revel in the stories of the woman who dares to challenge the men at her Ivy League university during the 1930s in *A Gentleman and a Scholar*, and another young woman who thumbs a lift and gets more than she bargained for in *A Wasted Hour* . . . plus ten other original tales.

JEFFREY ARCHER

TELL TALE

Complete and Unabridged

CHARNWOOD
Leicester

First published in Great Britain in 2017 by
Macmillan
an imprint of Pan Macmillan
London

First Charnwood Edition
published 2018
by arrangement with
Pan Macmillan
London

A catalogue record for this book is available
from the British Library.

ISBN 978–1–4448–3798–8

Published by
F. A. Thorpe (Publishing)
Anstey, Leicestershire

Set by Words & Graphics Ltd.
Anstey, Leicestershire
Printed and bound in Great Britain by
T. J. International Ltd., Padstow, Cornwall

This book is printed on acid-free paper

TO PAULA

My thanks to
Simon Bainbridge, Henry Colthurst,
Naresh Kumar, Christian Neffe,
Alison Prince, Catherine Richards,
Susan Watt and Maria Teresa Burgoni

Foreword

This is the first set of short stories I have written since the Clifton Chronicles.

Once again, some of them are loosely based on incidents that I've picked up on my travels from Grantchester to Calcutta, from Christchurch to Cape Town. These tales are marked with an asterisk, while the remainder are the result of my imagination.

Jeffrey Archer,
2017

Contents

* Inspired by real events

UNIQUE

A Challenge

Many years ago an editor from the *Reader's Digest* in New York invited me to write a hundred-word story with a beginning, a middle and an end. As if that wasn't enough of a challenge, he insisted that it couldn't be 99 words or 101.

Still not satisfied, he asked me to present the finished piece within twenty-four hours.

My first effort was 118 words, my second 106, and my third, 98. I wonder if you can work out which two words I had to put back in.

The result was 'Unique', which you will find on the next page.

It may interest readers to know, this is also 100 words.

Paris, 14 March 1921

The collector relit his cigar, picked up the magnifying glass and studied the triangular 1874 Cape of Good Hope.

'I did warn you there were two,' said the dealer, 'so yours is not unique.'

'How much?'

'Ten thousand francs.'

The collector wrote out a cheque, before taking a puff on his cigar, but it was no longer alight. He picked up a match, struck it, and set light to the stamp.

The dealer stared in disbelief as the stamp went up in smoke.

The collector smiled. 'You were wrong, my friend,' he said, 'mine is unique.'

WHO KILLED THE MAYOR?

Cortoglia is a delightfully picturesque town in the heart of Campania. It rests high on a hill, with commanding views towards Monte Taburno to the east, and Vesuvius to the south. It is described in *Fodor's Italy* quite simply as 'heaven on earth'.

The population of the town is 1,472, and hasn't varied greatly for over a century. The town's income is derived from three main sources: wine, olives and truffles. The Cortoglia White, aromatic with a vibrant acidity, is one of the most sought-after wines on earth and, because its production is limited, is sold out long before it's bottled. And as for the olive oil, the only reason you never see a bottle on the shelves of your local supermarket is because many of the leading Michelin-starred restaurants won't consider allowing any other brand on their premises.

The bonus, which allows the locals to enjoy a standard of living envied by their neighbours, is their truffles. Restaurateurs travel from all corners of the globe in search of the Cortoglia truffle, which is then only offered to their most discerning customers.

It is true that some people have been known to leave Cortoglia and seek their fortunes further afield, but the more sensible among them return fairly quickly. But then, life expectancy in the medieval hill town is eighty-six years for men and ninety-one for women, eight years above the national average.

In the centre of the main square is a statue of Garibaldi, now more famous for biscuits than battles, and the town boasts only a dozen shops, two restaurants and a wine bar. The council wouldn't sanction any more for fear it might attract tourists. There is no train service, and a bus appears in the town once a week for those foolish enough to wish to travel to Naples. A few of the residents own cars, but have little use for them.

The town is run by the *consiglio comunale*, made up of six elders. The most junior member, whose lineage only goes back three generations, is not considered by all to be a local. The owner of the winery, Lorenzo Pellegrino, chairman (ex officio), Paolo Caraffini, the manager of the olive oil company, and Pietro De Rosa, the truffle master, are all automatically members of the council, while the three remaining places come up for election every five years. As no one has stood against the schoolmaster, the pharmacist or the grocer for the past fifteen years, the voters have almost forgotten how to conduct an election.

The Polizia Locale had consisted of a single officer, Luca Gentile, whose authority derives from the city of Naples, and Luca tries not to disturb them unnecessarily. This story concerns the one occasion when it was necessary.

★　★　★

8

No one could be certain where Dino Lombardi had come from, but like a black cloud, he appeared overnight, and was clearly more interested in thunderstorms than showers. Lombardi must have been around six foot four, with the build of a heavyweight boxer who didn't expect his bouts to last for more than a couple of rounds.

He began his reign of terror with the weaker inhabitants of the town, the shopkeepers, the local tradesmen and the two restaurateurs, whom he persuaded needed protection, even if they couldn't be sure from whom, as there hadn't been a serious crime in Cortoglia in living memory. Even the Germans hadn't bothered to climb that particular hill.

To be fair, the policeman was going to retire soon, at the age of sixty-five, and the council hadn't got round to finding a replacement. But the real problem arose when the mayor, Mario Pellegrino, died at the age of 102, and an election had to be held to replace him.

It was assumed that his son Lorenzo would succeed him. Paolo Caraffini would then become chairman of the council, and everyone else would move up a place, with the vacancy being filled by Umberto Cattaneo, the local butcher. That was until Lombardi turned up at the town hall, and entered his name on the list for mayor. Of course, no one doubted Lorenzo Pellegrino would win by a landslide, so it came as something of a surprise when the town clerk, on crutches, his left leg in plaster, announced from the steps of the Palazzo dei Municipio that

9

Lombardi had polled 551 votes, to Pellegrino's 486. On hearing the result, there was a gasp of disbelief, not least because no one knew anyone who had voted for Lombardi.

Lombardi immediately took over the town hall, occupied the mayor's residence, and dismissed the council. He'd only been in office for a few days when the citizens learnt he would be imposing a sales tax on all three of the town's main companies, which was later extended to the shopkeepers and restaurateurs. And if that wasn't enough, he began to demand a kickback from the buyers as well as the sellers.

Within a year, heaven on earth had been turned into hell on earth, with the mayor quite happy to be cast in the role of Satan. So, frankly, it didn't come as a great shock to anyone when Lombardi was murdered.

Luca Gentile told the chairman of the council that as murder was out of his league, he would have to inform the authorities in Naples, and he admitted in his report that there were 1,472 suspects, and he had absolutely no idea who had committed the crime.

Naples, a city that knows a thing or two about murder, sent one of its brightest young detectives to investigate the crime, arrest the culprit and bring them back to the city to stand trial.

Antonio Rossetti, who, at the tender age of thirty-four, had recently been promoted to lieutenant, was assigned to the case, although he considered it an inconvenience that would keep him out of the front line — but surely not for long. He assured the chief of police that he

10

would wrap up the case as quickly as possible, and return to Naples so he could deal with some real criminals.

However, it didn't help that Luca Gentile died of a heart attack before Lieutenant Rossetti had set foot in Cortoglia. Some suggested Gentile was suffering from the strain of the whole affair, as the last murder in the town had been in 1892, when his great-grandfather had been the *poliziotto*. The only person left who seemed to know anything about the case was the examining doctor, who resided in the next village.

Rossetti called in to see Dr Barone on his way to Cortoglia. He was not pleased to discover that Lombardi had been cremated, and his ashes scattered on the far side of the mountain within hours of his death, such was the locals' hatred of the man. The one thing Dr Barone could confirm was that only he and Luca Gentile had seen the body before it was taken away in a plastic bag.

'So you and I are now the only people who know how the murder was committed,' said Barone as he handed over the results of the autopsy to Rossetti.

★ ★ ★

Lieutenant Antonio Rossetti arrived in Cortoglia later that evening, to be told that the council had decreed he should reside in the mayor's home until the murderer had been apprehended.

'After all,' the chairman said, 'let's get this over with so the young man can return to Naples as

11

quickly as possible.'

The following day, Antonio set up office in the local police station, which consisted of two small rooms, one unoccupied cell and a lavatory. After reading Dr Barone's report once again, he decided to leave his office and roam around the town, in the hope that someone might approach him wanting to offer information. But even though he walked slowly, and smiled a lot, people crossed the road rather than have to speak to him. He was clearly not looked upon as the Good Samaritan.

After a fruitless morning, Antonio returned to his office and made a list of those people who had most to gain from Lombardi's death. He came to the reluctant conclusion that he would have to start with the members of the town council. He wrote on his notepad, Wine, Oil and Truffles. He decided to start with Truffles, and called il Signor De Rosa's office to make an appointment to see the councillor later that afternoon.

★ ★ ★

'Would you care for a glass of wine?' said De Rosa, even before the policeman had sat down.

'No, thank you, sir, not while I'm on duty.'

'Quite right,' said De Rosa. Although it didn't stop him from pouring himself a large glass of the local white.

'Could we begin,' said Antonio, opening his notepad and looking down at his prepared questions. 'As your family have lived in Cortoglia

12

for over two hundred years — '

'Three hundred,' corrected the truffle master.

'I was hoping you might have an opinion on who killed Dino Lombardi?'

De Rosa refilled his glass and took a large gulp, before saying, 'I most certainly do, Lieutenant Rossetti, because I killed Lombardi.'

Antonio looked surprised. A confession on his second day. He was already thinking about returning to Naples in triumph, and getting back to locking up some serious criminals.

'Are you willing to sign a statement to that effect?'

'Most certainly I am.'

'And you do realize, Signor De Rosa, that you will have to come to Naples with me, stand trial and you may well spend the rest of your life in jail?'

'I have thought of little else since the day I killed the bastard. But I can't complain, I've had a good life.'

'Why did you murder Lombardi?' asked Antonio, who accepted that motive almost always accounted for any crime.

De Rosa filled his glass a third time. 'He was an evil man, Lieutenant, who terrified everyone who came into contact with him.' He paused, and took a sip of his wine, before adding, 'He made their lives unbearable, mine included.'

'How in particular?' Antonio persisted.

'He not only levied a crippling sales tax on my truffles, but then demanded backhanders from my oldest customers. If it had been allowed to go on for much longer, he would have put me out of

13

business.' Antonio kept on writing. 'Last year the company made a loss for the first time since I took over from my late father,' said De Rosa. 'The truth is, he got no more than he deserved.'

'I only have one more question,' the detective said. 'How did you kill him?'

'Stabbed him with my truffle knife,' said De Rosa without hesitation. 'It seemed appropriate.'

'And how many times did you stab him?'

'Six or seven,' he said, picking up a knife and giving a demonstration.

'I am sure you know, Signor De Rosa, it is a serious crime to waste police time.'

'Yes, of course I do,' said De Rosa, 'but now I have confessed, you can arrest me and lock me up.'

'I would be delighted to do so,' said Antonio, 'if only Lombardi had been stabbed.'

The truffle master shrugged his shoulders. 'Does it really matter? Just tell me how Lombardi was killed, and I'll confess to the crime.'

This was the first time Antonio had ever known someone admit to a crime they hadn't committed.

'I'm going to leave, Signor De Rosa, before you get yourself into even more trouble.'

The truffle master looked disappointed.

Antonio closed his notepad, stood up, and walked out of the room without another word. He tried not to laugh as he passed a pen full of the most contented pigs he'd ever seen, almost as if they knew they would never be slaughtered.

Antonio was on his way back to the police

station, when he spotted a pharmacy on the other side of the square, and remembered he needed a bar of soap and some tooth-paste. A little bell above the door rang as he stepped inside. He stood by the counter for a few moments, before a young woman came through from the dispensary, and said, 'Good morning, Signor Rossetti, how can I help you?'

When you're the only person in town that nobody knows, everyone knows you.

The hardest criminals from the back streets of Naples couldn't silence Antonio Rossetti, but a chemist from Cortoglia managed it with one sentence. She waited patiently for him to respond.

'I wanted a . . . bar of soap,' he eventually managed.

'You'll find there's quite a good selection behind you on the third shelf down.'

Antonio selected a bar, but ignored the toothpaste, because he wanted an excuse to return as soon as possible. He placed the soap on the counter and tried not to stare at her.

'Do the police expect to get everything free in Naples?' she asked, suppressing a smile.

'I'm so sorry,' said Antonio, quickly taking some coins out of his pocket and dropping them on the counter.

'Do come back if there's anything else you need,' she said, passing him a small bag.

He almost ran out of the shop and quickly returned to the police station. He sat in his office and began to write up a report on his abortive meeting with De Rosa, but found it hard to

15

concentrate. Once he'd done so, he returned to his list of names and crossed out Truffles.

Antonio decided he would next have to pay a visit to Paolo Caraffini, the owner of the olive oil company, but this time he wouldn't call to warn him. He left the police station just after lunch, and set out for the factory on the outskirts of town, pleased he would have to pass the pharmacy on the way. He slowed down as he approached the shop and glanced through the window. She was standing by the counter talking to an elderly woman, and looked up as he passed by. She smiled, which caused him to quicken his pace and hurry away.

When Antonio arrived at the Caraffini Olive Oil factory, he asked the receptionist if he could see il Signor Caraffini.

'Do you have an appointment?'

'No,' he said, and produced a warrant card.

'Yes, I know who you are,' said the receptionist. She picked up the phone and said, 'It's that policeman to see you.'

Antonio smiled, as a door on the other side of the corridor opened, and an elderly gentleman appeared. 'Do come in, Signor Rossetti,' he said graciously.

'I'm sorry I didn't make an appointment, sir,' Antonio said as he followed il Signor Caraffini into his office.

'That is quite understandable,' said Caraffini, 'after all, you were hoping to take me by surprise, whereas I am not at all surprised.'

'Why not?' asked Antonio as he sat down opposite him.

'Everyone knows you are investigating the murder of Lombardi, and I expected to be among the first people you would want to interview.'

'Why?'

'Because I've never hidden the fact I hated the man, and therefore assumed that the reason you didn't want to warn me is because you're about to arrest me.'

Antonio put down his pen. 'And why would I want to do that, Signor Caraffini?'

'Because it's common knowledge I killed the mayor, and I've been finding the strain of having to live with the crime almost unbearable.'

'Why did you kill him?'

'He was ruining my business. Another year of that damned man and there would have been nothing to leave to my children. I'm only thankful that my son is ready to take over now that I'll have to be locked up.' Caraffini stood up and stretched his arms across the desk as if expecting to be handcuffed.

'Before I arrest you, Signor Caraffini,' said the policeman, 'I am curious to know how you killed Lombardi?'

Caraffini didn't hesitate. 'I strangled him,' he said, before sitting back down.

'With what?'

This time he did hesitate. 'Does it matter?'

'Not really,' said Antonio, 'because I'm afraid Lombardi wasn't strangled.'

'But as he was cremated, how can you be so sure?'

'Because I've read the autopsy report, and I can assure you, Signor Caraffini, he wasn't strangled.'

'Tell me how he was killed, and I feel sure the murderer will give himself up fairly quickly, and that will solve all our problems.'

'It most certainly will not,' said Antonio. 'So be sure to tell your friends, Signor Caraffini, I'm going to catch whoever did murder Lombardi — and put them behind bars,' he added, as he slammed his notebook closed.

As Antonio got up to leave, he spotted a photograph on Caraffini's desk. The olive oil manager smiled. 'My daughter's wedding,' he explained. 'She married the son of my dear friend, Signor De Rosa. Oil and water may not mix, lieutenant, but olive oil and truffles certainly do.' He laughed at a joke Antonio presumed he'd made many times before.

'And the chief bridesmaid?' said Antonio, pointing to a young woman who was standing behind the bride.

'Francesca Farinelli, Signor Pellegrino's niece, who I had rather hoped would marry my second son, Mario, but it was not to be.'

'Why not?' said Antonio. 'That sounds an ideal match.'

'I agree. But modern Italian women seem to have minds of their own. I blame her father. He should never have let her go to university.' Antonio would have laughed, but he suspected the old man meant it. 'Only sorry I couldn't help you, Lieutenant.'

'So am I,' said Antonio.

The policeman decided to drop in to the pharmacy before he returned to his office to write up another abortive report. But he was disappointed to discover a middle-aged man standing behind the counter, chatting to a customer.

'How can I help you, Signor Rossetti?' he asked when he entered the shop.

'I need a tube of toothpaste.'

'Top shelf, on the right.'

He was just about to pay when Francesca appeared with a prescription.

'That should do the trick, signora. But do let me know if it gets any worse.'

'Thank you, my dear,' she said before leaving the shop.

'Have you come to arrest my father?' asked Francesca.

'No, at the moment I'm looking for someone who claims they didn't murder Lombardi.'

'Well, I'm sorry to say I didn't do it,' said il Signor Farinelli. 'I would happily have done so, but unfortunately I was in Rome attending a pharmaceutical conference that day.'

'But I wasn't,' said Francesca with a grin.

'It can't be much fun, holed up in a town where you don't know anyone,' said Farinelli.

'It could be worse,' said Antonio. 'The natives are starting to be friendly, and I certainly couldn't have better accommodation.'

'It's just that I wondered if you would care to join us for dinner one evening.'

'That's very kind of you.'

'Shall we say Thursday, around eight?'

'I'll look forward to it,' said Antonio as he turned to leave.

'Don't forget your toothpaste, Signor Rossetti,' said Francesca.

When Antonio turned up at the police station the following morning, there was a large, overweight man wearing a long blue-and-white striped apron standing outside the front door.

'Good morning, inspector.'

'Lieutenant,' corrected Antonio.

'I'm Umberto Cattaneo.'

'The butcher,' said Antonio. 'Your shop is in the town square?'

He nodded and lowered his voice. 'I think I may be able to help you with your enquiries.' At last, an informer, thought Antonio. He unlocked the door and led Cattaneo through to his little office. 'First, I need to be sure,' said Cattaneo, 'that if I tell you who killed Lombardi, it won't be traced back to me.'

'You have my word on that,' said Antonio, opening his notepad. 'That's assuming we won't need you to act as a witness when it comes to trial.'

'You won't need a witness,' said Cattaneo, 'because I can tell you where he's hidden the gun.'

Antonio snapped his notepad shut, and let out a deep sigh. 'But I haven't even told you who the murderer is,' said Cattaneo.

'You needn't bother, Signor Cattaneo, because Lombardi wasn't shot.'

'But Gian Lucio told me he'd shot him,' protested Cattaneo.

'Before I throw you in the cell and lock you up for a couple of days, if for no other reason than to stop your friends wasting my time, why are you happy to finger Gian Lucio for a crime he didn't commit?'

'Gian Lucio Altana is my oldest and dearest friend.'

'Then why are you trying to get him arrested?'

'I wasn't,' said Cattaneo. 'We tossed for it, and I lost.'

'You lost?'

'Whoever won got to say they killed Lombardi.'

'And how would you have killed Lombardi if you'd won the toss?'

'I would have shot him as well, and as we only have one pistol between us, we'd already agreed I would plant the gun at his place.'

'Just out of interest,' said Antonio, 'why was your friend Signor Altana so keen to admit he killed Lombardi?'

'While Lombardi was mayor, he'd eat at Lucio's restaurant three times a day.'

'That's hardly a good enough reason to kill a man.'

'It is when you lose all your regular customers because the mayor's always around.' Antonio nodded. 'By the way,' said Cattaneo, 'he wasn't stabbed, by any chance?'

'Get out of here, Signor Cattaneo, before I lock you and your friend up.'

Not a totally wasted morning, considered Antonio, because he was now confident only he, the doctor and the murderer had any idea how Lombardi had been killed.

21

★ ★ ★

Antonio knocked on the front door of Francesca's home a few minutes after eight. The door was opened by a middle-aged woman who greeted him with a warm smile.

'I'm Elena Farinelli, Francesca's mother. I've been looking forward to meeting you, Signor Rossetti. Please come in.' She led her guest through to the drawing room, where her husband was opening a bottle of wine. There was no sign of Francesca. 'She'll be down in a moment,' said Elena, almost as if she'd read his mind.

Mario Farinelli handed Antonio a glass, and asked, 'How many people have you arrested today?'

'It's been a little disappointing,' said Antonio. 'No one has admitted to killing Lombardi today,' he added as Francesca entered the room.

Antonio immediately realized it was the first time he'd seen her not wearing a long white coat. She was dressed in a red silk blouse, a black skirt and a pair of high-heeled shoes that certainly hadn't been bought in Cortoglia. He tried not to stare at her. What else was different? Of course, she'd let her hair down. He hadn't thought it possible that she could be even more beautiful.

'As you're a highly trained detective,' she said, 'I assume you already know my name is Francesca, but I don't know if you're Antonio or Tony?'

'My mother calls me Antonio, but my friends call me Tony.'

'I know you work in Naples,' said Elena Farinelli, 'but do your family also come from there?'

'Yes,' said Antonio, 'my parents are both schoolteachers, and I have two brothers. One's a printer and the other a lawyer.'

'Did you always want to be a policeman?' asked Francesca, as her father handed her a glass of wine.

'Yes I did. But then in Naples you have to work for one side of the law or the other.'

Everyone dutifully laughed, and Antonio was reminded how stilted conversations could be when you didn't know each other, but wanted to.

Francesca's mother turned out to be a traditional Italian housewife, whose cooking was so superb she could have opened her own restaurant. During dinner, her husband kept them all entertained with stories he'd overheard in the pharmacy. The biggest gossip shop in town, he admitted, and everyone had an opinion on who killed Lombardi.

'I have a feeling that by the time I get back to Naples, I'll be the only person who hasn't confessed to murdering the mayor.'

The Farinellis made it easy for Antonio to relax and feel at home, and he couldn't remember how many bottles of wine Mario had opened during the evening. But he was glad when the time came for him to leave that he could walk back to the mayor's house. If he'd driven, he would have had to arrest himself.

'See you tomorrow,' said Francesca, smiling, as she accompanied him to the front door. He looked puzzled. 'By then, it will surely be time for you to get another bar of soap. By the way, most of our customers buy them in boxes of three, even six.'

'Can I take you to dinner?' he asked.

'That would be nice.'

★ ★ ★

The day started badly for Antonio, when the postman felt it was his turn to confess to murdering the mayor.

'And how did you kill him, Signore?' he asked, not even picking up his pen.

'I drowned him,' said the postman.

'In the sea?' suggested Antonio, raising an eyebrow.

'No, in his bath. I took him by surprise.'

'You must have done,' said Antonio. 'But before I write down the details of your confession, may I ask, how tall are you?'

'I am five foot three and a half.'

'And you weigh?'

'Around one hundred and forty, one hundred and fifty pounds.'

'And you want me to believe you drowned a man of six foot four who weighed over three hundred pounds, and who some suggested never took a bath. Tell me, Signore, was he asleep at the time?'

'No,' said the postman, 'but he was drunk.'

'Ah, that would explain it,' said Antonio. 'But, frankly, if he'd been dead before you attempted to drown him, it would still have been a close-run thing.' The postman tried to look offended. 'Anyway, there's something else you've overlooked.'

'What's that?'

'Lombardi wasn't drowned. But good try, Signore, and more important, have I got any post this morning?'

'Yes, one from your mother, one from the chief of police in Naples, and another from your brother.'

'The printer or the lawyer?' Antonio asked as the postman placed the three letters on his desk.

'The lawyer.'

'Are there any secrets in this town?'

'Just one,' said the postman.

★　★　★

Dinner with Francesca at her favourite restaurant was about as public as an execution. If he'd even thought about holding her hand, it would have been front-page news in the *Cortoglia Gazzetta*.

'Don't you ever get bored living in a small town?' he asked her after a waiter had whisked away their plates.

'No,' she replied. 'I can read the same newspapers and the same books as you do, watch the same television programmes, eat the same food and drink the same wine. And if I want to buy some new clothes, visit an art gallery, or go to the opera, I can always spend the day in Naples.'

'But the bustle, the excitement, the — '

'The traffic, the pollution, and the graffiti, not

to mention the manners of some of your fellow Neapolitans.'

'I want to hold your hand,' he said, while the Beatles record played in the background.

Francesca looked around the tables and smiled. 'Then we'd better skip dessert and go for a walk.'

'I'll settle the bill,' said Antonio, taking out his wallet.

'There won't be a bill,' said Francesca. 'Gian Lucio is telling everyone that although he confessed to killing the mayor, you refused to arrest him.'

'Because he wasn't guilty,' protested Antonio. When they stood up to leave, Gian Lucio bustled across to say he hoped he would see them both again before too long.

As they walked together through a maze of cobbled streets, Francesca chatted as if they were old friends, another new experience for Antonio. And when they finally ended up outside her front door, they kissed for the first time.

'See you tomorrow,' Francesca said as she put her key in the lock. 'Will it be razor blades or shaving cream I wonder?'

She had closed the door before he could reply.

★ ★ ★

The Naples chief of police called Antonio at the end of the month, and asked if he was making any progress.

'Can't pretend I am, chief,' admitted Antonio. 'To date,' he said, opening a thick file,

26

'thirty-three people have confessed to killing Lombardi, and what makes it worse, I think they all know who did.'

'Someone will crack,' said the chief. 'They always do.'

'This isn't Naples, chief,' he heard himself saying.

'So who's the latest one?'

'Not one, eleven. The local football team are claiming they pushed Lombardi over a cliff.'

'And what makes you so sure they didn't?'

'I interviewed all eleven of them separately, and they couldn't even agree on which part of the cliff they pushed him over, or how they got him back to his house and tucked him up in bed. And in any case, I can tell you they're just not murderers.'

'How can you be so sure, Antonio?'

'They haven't won a match in the past fifteen years. In any case, that wasn't how Lombardi was killed.'

'He's clearly not going to be missed by anyone,' said the chief, 'because I've just received a report from my Head of Organized Crime, and it seems the Camorra expelled him because they thought he was too violent. So if you're no nearer to solving the crime by the end of next month, I want you back in Naples where real murderers are still roaming the streets.'

★ ★ ★

Everyone took the day off, Antonio included, to celebrate the installation of the new mayor.

27

Lorenzo Pellegrino was elected unopposed, which didn't come as a surprise to anyone, and the council of six remained in place. Dancing and drinking in the town square went on until the early hours, right outside Antonio's bedroom window, and that wasn't the only reason he couldn't get to sleep.

The next morning he called his mother to tell her he'd met the woman he wanted to marry, and she would be captivated, and not just by her beauty.

'I can't wait to meet her,' said his mother. 'Why don't you bring her to Naples for the weekend?'

'Why don't you and Papa come to Cortoglia?'

★ ★ ★

During the next month, the number of citizens who confessed to killing Lombardi rose from thirty-three to forty-one, and when the chief called again from Naples, Antonio had to admit that the locals had defeated him, and he accepted that perhaps the time had come to close the case and head back to the real world.

Indeed, Antonio might have done so if the new mayor hadn't phoned and asked to see him on a private matter. As the young detective walked across the square to the town hall, he assumed that the number of murderers in the town was about to rise from forty-one to forty-two, as Pellegrino was now the only person on the council who hadn't confessed to murdering Lombardi. But when the town clerk met him at the top, no longer on crutches, and accompanied him to the council chamber, he found the mayor and all six councillors sitting in their places, clearly waiting for him.

Antonio sat down at the other end of the table and as every member of the council had already admitted to killing Lombardi, together or separately, he wasn't sure why he'd been summoned.

'Signor Rossetti,' began the mayor. 'We've just held a meeting of the *consiglio comunale*, and have unanimously agreed to offer you the post of police chief.' But you only usually have one policeman, Antonio wanted to remind him. 'We've checked how much the Naples chief of police is paid, and we've agreed to equal it, and we also feel, with so many murderers on the loose, you will need a deputy.'

'That's very generous, but — '

'We also accept that the time has come to build a new police station, that's worthy of the town.'

'I agree that's none too soon, but — '

'And I'm quite happy for you to go on living in the mayor's house,' said Pellegrino, 'because I certainly don't need two homes.'

The third, 'But . . . ' wasn't quite as insistent.

'And,' continued the mayor, 'although we didn't put it to a vote, if you felt able to marry a local girl, I think that would go down well.'

★ ★ ★

Several guests arrived from Naples on the morning of the wedding, but Antonio assured

29

the mayor they would all be going home the next day.

The whole town turned out to witness the vows of eternal love sworn by Antonio Rossetti and Francesca Farinelli, including several who hadn't been invited. When il Signor and la Signora Rossetti left the wedding celebrations to set off for Venice, Antonio suspected the festivities would still be going on when they returned in a fortnight's time.

The newly-weds spent their honeymoon eating too much spaghetti alle vongole, and drinking too much wine, while still finding a way of not putting on too much weight.

On the last day of the honeymoon, they both confessed they were looking forward to getting back to Cortoglia. After a memorable meal at Harry's Bar, they took a gondola back to the Cipriani, to spend their last night together in Venice.

Antonio sat up in bed and watched his wife undress, and when she slipped under the covers to join him, he took her in his arms.

'Thank you for the most wonderful fortnight,' said Francesca, 'but most of all for not once mentioning Lombardi.'

Antonio smiled. 'You're about the only person I haven't asked who you think killed him.'

'I did,' said Francesca, snuggling closer.

Antonio laughed. 'And how did you kill him, my darling?'

'I poisoned him. Two drops of cyanide in his coffee just before he went to bed,' Francesca said as she turned out the bedside light.

Antonio froze.

VIEW OF AUVERS-SUR-OISE

'It's like making love for the first time,' said the chief inspector. 'A copper never forgets his first arrest.'

While all his chums at school wanted to be Han Solo or James Bond, Guy Stanford saw himself more as Sherlock Holmes. So when the careers master asked him what he wanted to do when he left school, no one was surprised when he replied, 'I'm going to be a detective.'

Guy's only problem was his father, who assumed that like him, he would train to be a barrister and later join him in chambers. Being English, they agreed on a compromise. And as with parents who are unsure their son is marrying the right girl, Guy agreed to a trial separation; if he still felt the same way about it after three years, his father would put up no objection to him joining the police force.

Guy spent the next three years at Exeter University studying the history of art — the second love of his life. He graduated with a good enough honours degree for his tutor to suggest he might consider returning to do a PhD thesis on Sorolla, the Spanish impressionist. Guy thanked his tutor, took the next train back to Coventry, and after a two-week holiday, joined the local police force.

Guy didn't take advantage of the graduate entry scheme that guaranteed accelerated promotion because, as he told his father, he preferred to win his spurs on the battlefield. His four years on the beat before he became a detective turned out to be full of challenges. For example . . . no. This is not a story about the recently promoted Chief Superintendent Guy Stanford, but a tale about PC Stanford's first arrest.

It had been a particularly gruelling week for Guy, which had ended on Saturday afternoon with his having to accompany the visiting Cardiff City football supporters back to the station, after they'd lost to Coventry, 3 — 0.

Once the last train had departed, Guy decided not to join his mates at the pub that evening, but to curl up in bed with a good book. But he was so exhausted that he only managed a couple of chapters of *Duveen* by S. N. Behrman before he fell into a deep sleep.

Twenty minutes later his dreams were interrupted by an insistent ringing. But it was still some time before he managed to pick up the phone.

'Stanford,' said a voice that wasn't used to being disobeyed. 'Report to the station immediately. And immediately means you're already late.'

'Yes, sarge,' said Guy, suddenly wide awake. He leapt out of bed, took a two-minute shower, didn't shave and threw on his uniform. He ran downstairs and out onto the street, jumped on his bike and didn't stop pedalling until he reached the station.

Once he'd dumped the bike, he joined several of his colleagues who were charging up the steps into the nick.

'Downstairs, lads,' said the desk sergeant. An order Guy obeyed without stopping.

When he entered the large situations room in the basement, he joined thirty or forty of his colleagues who had clearly all been drafted in at short notice. Although none of them had any idea what they were doing there, they didn't have to wait long to find out.

When Chief Superintendent Dexter (crime) walked in, Guy realized it had to be serious, and when the chief constable followed only a pace behind, the whole room fell silent.

'OK, listen up, lads,' said the super, as he placed his hands on his hips, 'because I don't have time to repeat myself. A small inner group of senior police officers have been working for several weeks on a particularly sensitive investigation. However, I was unwilling to give the go-ahead until we were confident every piece of the jigsaw was in place. An hour ago, we received information from a reliable source that we wouldn't get a better opportunity than tonight to bang up Bernie Manners, along with a few other well-known villains.'

Several of the officers began to cheer and applaud. Although Guy hadn't come in contact with Manners, he knew only too well who he was. His photograph had become a dartboard in the crime room long before Guy had joined the force. He knew Manners was the local drug baron, who controlled a territory that stretched from Watford to Birmingham, and anyone who strayed onto his patch went missing. But far worse were the number of young lives he had ruined with the distribution of heroin and crack cocaine by his army of dealers. Thanks to a cadre of expensive lawyers, Manners had never been convicted or seen the inside of a prison cell. Even when they'd found a shotgun in the boot of his Mercedes, Manners was able to prove he was on the way to a pheasant shoot, and that the gun was registered. The jury didn't seem to understand the difference between a shotgun and a rifle.

'My informant tells me,' continued the super, 'that Manners is holding a party in his home tonight to celebrate his fiftieth birthday, and among his guests will be some of the biggest rogues in Christendom, so we'll never get a better opportunity to give him an unexpected birthday present.'

This time the cheer was even louder.

'All of you will now be divided into three groups with a senior officer in charge of each section. Group one will be under my orders and will act as the lead unit. Group two will consist of twenty-one officers under Chief Inspector Wallis, who will surround the house, and if you find as much as a half-smoked joint on anyone trying to beat a hasty retreat, arrest them, bring them back to the nick and lock 'em up. Group three, you're the search party and will be led by Chief Inspector Hendry. Once you get the signal from me, you will enter the house, where you will each be allocated a room, and then I expect you to take the place apart. Any drugs you find must be listed, bagged and handed over to Inspector Hendry.'

Guy looked around to see that most of his colleagues couldn't wait to get going. This was the reason they'd joined the police.

'And don't forget. Every ounce of heroin or coke you find is another year in jail for Manners, and it's a life sentence if we can prove he's a dealer. Right, report to your group commanders who will brief you more fully.'

There was almost a stampede towards a large notice board where every officer was listed in alphabetical order, showing which group they had been allocated to.

Guy knew he wasn't senior enough to be a member of the command unit, but he still wanted to be in the search party, and not left standing outside the house hoping someone would try to do a runner.

He let out a muted 'Yes!', when he saw the number 3 by his name, and quickly made his way back upstairs and out of the nick. He climbed into a black patrol van, marked only with the number 3, and took a seat near the front. Once the door of the van slid shut, Chief Inspector Hendry began to brief his group.

'Right, pay attention. Like the chief, I'm only going to say this once. Our job will be to search the house from top to bottom, making sure we don't miss anything, and I mean anything. If you come across any drugs, even marijuana or poppers, bag them up and bring them straight to me. Don't expect to find everything stacked and labelled neatly on shelves. Manners will have stashed them in places you won't even have thought of, so make sure you do a thorough job, because we're not going to get a second chance.'

Guy looked out of the window as the convoy moved off. He was in the third of three unmarked vans, with two patrol cars in front leading the way, and another two behind bringing up the rear. They were clearly expecting a lot of guests at the party.

The convoy drove silently out of the city, ignoring drunks and vagrants who quickly disappeared down unlit alleys the moment they saw them. And once they'd crossed the city boundary and began to drive through neighbouring villages, Guy noticed that few lights were still on, as most civilized people were already in bed, sound asleep.

With about a mile to go, Hendry stood up, turned to face his group and said, 'Look lively, lads, it won't be long now.'

As they swung off the main road, the two police cars in front turned off their headlights and parked down a narrow lane. Guy looked out of the window to see a vast Georgian mansion lit only by the full moon. In fact the first thing Guy noted was that there wasn't a light on in the house. If Bernie Manners was holding a party to celebrate his fiftieth birthday, he found it hard to believe the guests had already gone home.

When the convoy came to a halt, Guy and his colleagues sat waiting impatiently for the off. But in which direction, wondered Guy. He assumed the senior officers sitting in the first van were discussing whether to go ahead with the operation or slink back to the station, tails between their legs and admit they'd been sold a bum steer. In Guy's opinion that would have been the most sensible thing to do. But he knew Chief Superintendent Dexter only had a few months to go before he retired, and no doubt that was also being weighed in the balance. What a scalp to end his career with.

And then it became obvious what decision had been made, because the two police cars in front switched their headlights back on and began to move slowly up the drive towards the house. Guy watched as his colleagues poured out of the vans and began to surround the building, while Hendry led his team off the third van and onto the front lawn. He raised an arm and his group stopped, just yards from the front door.

No one moved when the super banged a clenched fist on the door. Moments later, a light shone from a second-floor window, followed by another on the stairs, and finally one in the hallway, before the front door was opened to reveal the massive figure of Bernie Manners framed in the doorway, adorned in a purple silk dressing gown.

'What's the meaning of this intrusion, Chief Superintendent?' demanded Manners.

Guy's immediate reaction was, why wasn't Manners surprised when he saw Dexter standing on his front doorstep? And why no shouting or bad language? Guy was beginning to wonder if the reliable source had always been working for the other side, but it was too late to turn back now.

'I have a warrant to search these premises,' said the superintendent, who handed over a court document for Manners to study, and he didn't wait to be invited in. Guy knew the warrant would have been issued by a judge earlier that evening, no doubt with a warning of the consequences if they didn't come up with a substantial cache of drugs that couldn't be described by a seasoned lawyer as recreational.

A few minutes later, the super reappeared in the doorway and waved a beckoning hand. The sign for the search party to join him in the house.

'OK, lads, let's get moving,' said Hendry as he led his men across the gravel courtyard and into the house.

Guy and two other officers were ordered to search the drawing room. To start with, they satisfied themselves with checking inside drawers, removing cushions from the sofas and chairs, and pulling books, CDs and DVDs from the shelves above the widescreen television. Inspector Hendry moved from room to room waiting for the first officer to report a find, while Manners poured himself a drink. An hour later the CO gave the order to move on to what he described as a more thorough search.

'You ain't gonna find a damn thing,' said Manners. 'Not that I have any idea what you're looking for,' he added as he poured himself another large whisky.

Guy believed the first statement, but not the second. The young constable switched his attention back to the job in hand, as a sergeant unsheathed a knife and thrust the blade deep into the sofa, causing feathers to fly in every direction. Guy started to remove the few books from the shelves and began to sift through the

40

pages, but all he came up with was a fifty-pound note that had been used as a bookmark — not a crime.

The second hour also yielded nothing, except the downstairs rooms now resembled a council rubbish dump, and it worried Guy that Manners didn't seem to care. In fact he was beginning to wonder just who had planned this whole operation months in advance.

Manners put down his drink, checked his watch and made a phone call. It wasn't difficult for Guy to work out who he'd be calling at that time of night, but he was surprised how quickly the phone was answered.

In desperation, the super gave orders for everyone to change floors, and double-check their colleagues hadn't missed anything.

Guy was allocated the bathroom. He made his way slowly up to the first floor, taking a moment to look at the paintings on the wall that were, with one exception, second-rate dross, probably bought from the railings on Piccadilly by an interior decorator who knew a sucker when he saw one.

He moved into the bathroom, which resembled a rugby changing room after a hard-fought game, and it only took him a few moments to realize his colleagues had done a thorough job, even removing the panels from the side of the bath and checking behind a medicine cabinet filled with drugs from Boots. But search as he might, Guy couldn't come up with anything stronger than an aspirin.

They all heard the whistle, the sign that the

41

search was being called off. Guy came slowly back down the stairs to see the super looking as if he might be facing an earlier retirement than he had originally anticipated, but Guy now suspected that was all part of Manners' plan. Bang on cue, a black BMW came up the drive and double-parked outside the front door.

A moment later a tall, elegantly dressed man marched into the house, looking as if he hadn't been to bed.

'Michael,' said Manners. 'I wanted you to see what these bastards have been up to,' he added before he took his lawyer on a tour of the house so he could survey the carnage. When they reappeared, the man walked straight across to the chief superintendent and said, 'My name is Michael Carstairs.'

'I know exactly who you are, Mr Carstairs.'

'And I have the privilege of representing Mr Manners,' he continued as if he hadn't been interrupted, 'whose home you have ransacked for no apparent reason, especially as you must be well aware that my client is a respected local businessman, who has resided in the area for many years. So I'm sure you won't be surprised that I shall be making an official complaint on his behalf, but not before I've spoken to the chief constable.'

Guy watched carefully to see how the super would react. Dexter looked as if he couldn't be sure which of the two men to punch first, the lawyer or his client. At least if he had, he would have something to show for his troubles.

'If you're not going to charge my client with

any offence,' continued Carstairs, 'perhaps it's time for you and your thugs to get out.'

The chief superintendent was about to give the order for his men to leave the premises, when Guy stepped forward.

'And what have we here?' said Carstairs, staring at the fresh-faced young constable standing in front of his client. 'Are you by any chance the arresting officer?'

'Yes, I am,' said Guy.

Manners burst out laughing, while the lawyer added contemptuously, 'On what charge, dare I ask?'

'Possession of stolen goods.'

'No doubt you're able to substantiate your wild claim, Constable,' he said, making no attempt to mask any sarcasm.

'I most certainly can,' said Guy, before he began to climb back up the stairs while his colleagues watched nervously. He stopped halfway, and removed an oil painting from the wall before coming back down to the hall.

'Do you recognize this painting, Mr Manners?' asked Guy, holding it up in front of him.

Manners just stood there, looking at his lawyer.

'It's a Cézanne,' said Guy. 'He was one of the most influential artists of the early twentieth century.' Guy paused to admire the painting. 'Never signed or dated, because the artist considered *View of Auvers-sur-Oise* unfinished, but more interesting is that the painting was stolen from the Ashmolean Museum in Oxford the night before the Millennium.' Guy turned to face the lawyer. 'I wonder if you have any idea of its value, Mr Carstairs?'

The lawyer didn't offer an opinion.

'Sotheby's valued it at a little over three million, but that's possibly a conservative estimate, as Sir Nicholas Serota, the director of the Tate, described the painting as a national treasure, and irreplaceable.'

The chief superintendent nodded, and two of his senior officers stepped forward, handcuffed Manners, read him his rights, and led him out to a waiting car. Guy reluctantly handed over the painting to the chief superintendent.

As Hendry caught up with Guy on his way back to the van, the chief inspector remarked, 'It's like making love for the first time, lad. A copper never forgets his first arrest.'

A GENTLEMAN AND
A SCHOLAR

When she entered the lecture theatre for the last time, the entire faculty rose and cheered. She progressed up the steps and onto the stage, feigning to be unaffected by their warm reception. She waited for her students to resume their places before she began to deliver her final lecture.

She held her emotions in check as she looked up at the assembled audience for the first time. A lecture theatre that held three hundred and was rarely full was now so packed with professors, lecturers and scholars she had taught over the past four decades, that some of them had spilled out onto the steps at the sides, while others stood hugger-mugger at the back.

Many had travelled from across the nation to sit at her feet and acknowledge the curtain coming down on an illustrious career. But as she stood and looked at them, Professor Burbage couldn't help recalling it hadn't always been that way.

★ ★ ★

Margaret Alice Burbage had studied English literature at Radcliffe before sailing across the ocean to spend a couple of years at the other Cambridge, where she completed a PhD on Shakespeare's early sonnets.

Dr Burbage was offered the chance to remain

47

in Cambridge as a teaching fellow at Girton, but declined as she wished to return to her native land, and like a disciple spreading the Gospel, preach about the Bard of Stratford-upon-Avon to her fellow countrymen.

Although vast areas of America had become emancipated, there still remained a small group of universities who were not quite ready to believe a woman could teach a man — anything. Among the worst examples of these heathens were Yale and Princeton, who did not allow women to darken their doors until 1969.

In 1970, when Dr Burbage applied for the position of assistant professor at Yale, she told her mother after being interviewed by the all-male panel that she had no hope of being offered the post, and indeed, she expected to return to Amersham, where she would happily teach English at the local girls' school where she had been educated. But to everyone's surprise, other than that of the interviewing panel, she was offered the position, albeit at two-thirds of the salary of her male colleagues.

Questions were whispered in the cloisters as to where she would go to the lavatory, who would cover for her when she was having her period, and even who would sit next to her in the dining room.

Several former alumni made their feelings clear to the president of Yale, and some even moved their offspring to other universities lest they be contaminated, while another more active group were already plotting her downfall.

When Dr Burbage had entered the same

theatre some forty-two years before to deliver her first lecture, the troops were lined up and ready for battle. As she walked onto that same stage, she was greeted by an eerie silence. She looked up at the 109 students, who were ranged in the amphitheatre around her like lions who'd spotted a stray Christian.

Dr Burbage opened her notebook and began her lecture.

'Gentlemen,' she said, as there weren't any other ladies in the room, 'my name is Margaret Burbage, and I shall be giving twelve lectures this term, covering the canon of William Shakespeare.'

'But did he even write the plays?' said a voice who didn't attempt to make himself known.

She looked around the tiered benches, but wasn't able to identify which of the students had addressed her.

'There's no conclusive proof that anyone else wrote the plays,' she said, abandoning her prepared notes, 'and indeed —'

'What about Marlowe?' another voice demanded.

'Christopher Marlowe was unquestionably one of the leading playwrights of the day, but in 1593 he was killed in a bar-room brawl, so —'

'What does that prove?' Yet another voice.

'That he couldn't have written *Richard II*, *Romeo and Juliet*, *Hamlet* or *Twelfth Night*, all of which were penned after Marlowe's death.'

'Some say Marlowe wasn't killed, but to escape the law, went to live in France, where he wrote the plays, sent them back to England, and allowed his friend Shakespeare to take the credit.'

'For those who indulge in conspiracy theories, that rates alongside believing the moon landings were set up in a TV studio somewhere in Nebraska.'

'The same doesn't apply to the Earl of Oxford.' Another voice.

'Edward de Vere, the seventeenth Earl of Oxford, was unquestionably a well-educated and accomplished scholar, but unfortunately he died in 1604, so he couldn't have written *Othello*, *Macbeth*, *Coriolanus* or *King Lear*, arguably Shakespeare's greatest work.'

'Unless Oxford wrote them before his death.' The same voice.

'There can't be many playwrights who, having written nine masterpieces, then leave them to languish in their bottom drawer and forget to mention them to anyone, including the producers and theatre owners of the day, one of whom, Edward Parsons, we know paid Shakespeare six pounds for *Hamlet*, because the British Museum has the receipt to prove it.'

'Henry James, Mark Twain and Sigmund Freud wouldn't agree with you.' Another voice.

'Neither would Orson Welles, Charlie Chaplin or Marilyn Monroe,' said Dr Burbage, 'and perhaps more interesting, they were unable to agree with one another.'

One young man had the grace to laugh.

'Can Francis Bacon be dismissed quite so easily? After all, he was born before Shakespeare, and died after him, so at least the dates fit.'

'Which is about the only thing that does,' said Dr Burbage. 'However, I acknowledge without question that Bacon was a true Renaissance man. What we would today call a polymath. A talented writer, an able lawyer, and a brilliant philosopher, who ended up as Lord Chancellor of England during the reign of King James I. But the one thing Bacon doesn't seem to have managed during his busy career was to write a play, let alone thirty-seven.'

'Then how do you explain that Shakespeare left school at fourteen, was not well versed in Latin, and somehow managed to write *Hamlet* without visiting Denmark, not to mention half a dozen plays set in Italy, having never set foot outside of England?'

'Only five of Shakespeare's plays are set in Italy,' she said, landing her first blow. 'And scholars also accept that neither Marlowe nor Oxford, or even Bacon, ever visited Denmark.' Which seemed to send her recalcitrant pupils into retreat, allowing her to add, 'However, the distinguished satirist, Jonathan Swift, who was born a mere fifty years after Shakespeare's death, put it so much better than I could:

'*When a true genius appears in the world, you may know him by this sign, that the dunces are all in confederacy against him.*'

As that seemed to silence them, Dr Burbage felt she had won the first skirmish, but suspected the battalions were reforming before they launched an all-out attack.

'How important is it to have a good knowledge of the text?' asked someone who at least had the courtesy to raise a hand so she could identify him.

'Most important,' said Dr Burbage, 'but not as important as being able to interpret the meaning of the words, so you have a better understanding of the text.'

Assuming the battle was over, she returned to her lecture notes. 'During this semester, I shall require you all to read one of the history plays, a comedy and a tragedy, and at least ten sonnets. Although you may make your own selection, I shall expect you, by the end of term, to be able to quote at length from the plays and sonnets you have chosen.'

'If we were to, between us, select every play and every sonnet, could you also quote at length from the entire canon?' The first voice again.

Dr Burbage looked down at the names on the seating plan in front of her and identified Mr Robert Lowell, whose grandfather had been a former president of Yale.

'I consider myself familiar with most of Shakespeare's work, but like you, Mr Lowell, I am still learning,' she said, hoping this would keep him in his place.

Lowell immediately stood, clearly the leader of the rebels. 'Then perhaps you would allow me to test that claim, Dr Burbage.' And before she could tell the young man to sit down and stop showing off, he added, 'Shall we begin with something easy?

'Our revels now are ended. These our actors,
As I foretold you, were all spirits and

Are melted into air, into thin air.
And, like the baseless fabric of this vision,
The cloud-capp'd towers, the gorgeous palaces,
The solemn temples, the great globe itself —'

Dr Burbage was impressed that he didn't once look down at the text, so she obliged him and took up where he had left off.

'*Yea, all which it inherit, shall dissolve,*
And, like this insubstantial pageant faded,
Leave not a rack behind. We are such stuff
As dreams are made on, and our little life
Is rounded with a sleep.'

One or two of the students nodded when she added, '*The Tempest*, act four, scene one.' But Lowell was right, he'd begun with something easy. Their leader sat down to allow a lieutenant to take his place, who looked equally well prepared.

'*Give every man thy ear, but few thy voice;*
Take each man's censure, but reserve thy
judgement.
Costly thy habit as thy purse can buy,
But not express'd in fancy; rich, not gaudy;
For the apparel oft proclaims the man,'

the lieutenant recited, his eyes never leaving her, but she didn't flinch.

'*And they in France of the best rank and*
station

53

Are most select and generous, chief in that.
Neither a borrower nor a lender be;
For loan oft loses both itself and friend,
And borrowing dulls the edge of husbandry.
This above all: to thine own self be true,
And it must follow, as the night the day,
Thou canst not then be false to any man.

'Hamlet, act one, scene three.'

It was now clear to her that several among their dwindling ranks were not only following the text word for word in open books, but then turning a few pages clearly aware where the next volley would come from, and although another foot soldier had been shot down, someone quite happily rose to take his place. But this one looked as if he'd have been more at home on a football field, and read directly from the text.

'There shall be in England seven halfpenny
loaves sold for a penny: the three-hooped
pot shall have ten hoops and I will make it
felony to drink small beer. All the realm
shall be in common; and in Cheapside
shall my palfrey go to grass.'

Dr Burbage had to concentrate as it had been some time since she'd read *Henry VI*. She hesitated for a moment while everyone's eyes remained fixed on her. A flicker of triumph appeared on Mr Lowell's face.

'And when I am king, as king I will be,
there shall be no money: all shall eat and

*drink on my score; and I will apparel them
all in one livery, that they may agree like
brothers, and worship me their lord.*

'Henry VI, Part Two — ' She couldn't remember the act or scene, so to cover herself immediately said, 'But can you tell me the next line?'

A blank look appeared on the young man's face, and he clearly wanted to sit down.

'*"The first thing we do"*,' said Dr Burbage, '*"let's kill all the lawyers."*'

This was greeted with laughter and a smattering of applause, as the questioner sank back in his place. But they hadn't given up yet, because another foot soldier quickly took his place.

'*Now is the winter of our discontent — *'

'Too easy, move on,' she said, as another soldier bit the dust to allow the next brave soul to advance over his fallen comrades. But one look at this particular young man, and Dr Burbage knew she was in trouble. He was clearly at home on the battlefield, his bayonet fixed, and ready for the charge. He spoke softly, without once referring to the text.

'*Take but degree away, untune that sting,
And, hark, what discord follows! Each thing
    meets . . . *'

She couldn't remember the play the lines were from, and she certainly wasn't able to complete the verse, but he'd made a mistake which just might rescue her.

'Wrong word,' she said firmly. 'Not sting, but string. Next?' she added, confident that no one would doubt she could have delivered the next four lines. She would have to look up the scene once she was back in the safety of her room.

Dr Burbage stared defiantly down at a broken army in retreat, but still their commanding officer refused to surrender. Lowell stood among the fallen, undaunted, unbowed, but she suspected he only had one bullet left in his barrel.

'The painful warrior famoused for fight,
After a thousand victories once foil'd — '

She smiled, and said:

' *— Is from the book of honour razed quite,*
And all the rest forgot for which he toil'd.

Can you tell me the number of the sonnet, Mr Lowell?'

Lowell just stood there, like a man facing the firing squad, as his fallen comrades looked on in despair. But in her moment of triumph, Margaret Alice Burbage allowed her pride to get the better of her.

''*I would challenge you to a battle of wits,*' Mr Lowell, '*but I see you are unarmed.*''

The students burst out laughing, and she felt ashamed.

Professor Burbage looked down at her class.

'If I may be allowed to leave you with a single thought,' she said. 'It has been my life's mission to introduce fertile and receptive minds to the greatest poet and playwright that ever lived in the tide of times. However, I have come to realize in old age that Will was also the greatest storyteller of them all, and in this, my final lecture, I shall attempt to make my case.

'If we had all been visiting London in 1595, when I would have been a whore or a lady-in-waiting — often the same thing . . . ' Professor Burbage had to wait for the laughter to die down before she could continue, 'I would have taken you to the Globe Theatre on Cheapside to see the Lord Chamberlain's Men, and for a penny, we could have stood among a thousand groundlings to watch my great ancestor Richard Burbage give you his Romeo. Of course we would have marvelled at the poetry, been entranced by the verse, but I would suggest that it would have been the tale that would have had you on the edge of your seats as we all waited to find out what was going to happen to our hero and his Juliet. What modern playwright would dare to poison the heroine, only to bring her back to life to find her lover, thinking she was dead, has taken his own life, and she, no longer wanting to live, stabs herself? Of course, we are all familiar with the story of Romeo and Juliet, but if there are those among you who have not read all thirty-seven plays, or

57

seen them performed, you now have a unique opportunity to find out if I'm right. However, I wouldn't bother with *The Two Noble Kinsmen*, as I'm not altogether convinced Shakespeare wrote it.'

She looked at her enthralled audience, and waited only for a moment before she broke the spell.

'On a higher note, I would also suggest that if Shakespeare were alive today, Hollywood would insist on a happy ending to *Romeo and Juliet*, with the two star-crossed lovers standing on the prow of Drake's *Golden Hind* staring out into the sunset.'

It was some time before the laughter and applause died down, and she was able to continue.

'And as for the politically correct, what would the *New York Times* have made of a fourteen-year-old boy having sex with a thirteen-year-old girl on Broadway?'

While the professor waited for the applause to die down, she turned the last page of her notes.

'And so, ladies and gentlemen, despite this being my final lecture, you will not escape without attempting the Burbage witch test to discover who among you is a genuine scholar.' An exaggerated groan went up around the room, which she ignored. 'I shall now read a couplet from one of Shakespeare's plays, in the hope that one of the brighter ones among you will give me the next three lines.' She looked up and smiled at her audience, to be met with apprehensive looks.

'*For time is like a fashionable host*
That slightly shakes his parting guest by the
  hand.'

A silence followed, and Professor Burbage allowed herself a moment to enjoy the thought that she had defeated young and old alike in her final lecture, until a tall, distinguished-looking gentleman rose slowly from his place near the back of the auditorium. Although she hadn't seen him for over forty years, Margaret knew exactly who he was. Now gaunt of face, with grey hair, and a severed arm from war to remind her that he wasn't someone who retreated in the face of the enemy.

'*And with his arms outstretch'd, as he would*
  fly,
Grasps in the comer: the welcome ever smiles,
And farewell goes out sighing,'

he offered in a voice she could never forget.
  'Which play?' she demanded.
  '*Troilus and Cressida,*' he said confidently.
  'Correct. But for your bonus, which act and which scene?'
  He hesitated for a moment before saying, 'Act three, scene two.'
  It was the right act but the wrong scene, but Professor Burbage simply smiled and said, 'You're quite right, Mr Lowell.'

ALL'S FAIR IN LOVE AND WAR

Ralph — pronounced Raif — Dudley Dawson became squire of the village of Nethercote when his father died. After all, his father and grandfather had always been addressed as 'squire' by the locals, and as he'd inherited Nethercote Hall, with its thousand acres of farmland and ten thousand sheep, he rather assumed he'd be treated with the same deference. So convinced was Ralph of his birthright, he refused to open letters that weren't addressed to Ralph Dudley Dawson Esq.

Any friends Ralph had, of whom there were few, were either richer than he was or listed in *Debrett's*, and, like the Royal Family, he considered it nothing less than his duty to marry someone from his own class, or preferably even higher. After all, Ralph was a good catch.

The only problem for Ralph was that he didn't come across too many young women living in the depths of Cornwall who fitted the bill. The lord lieutenant of the county, Sir Miles Seymour, had three daughters: Arabella, who was beautiful, Charlotte, who was charming, and Clare, who was neither, but inexplicably all three turned him down. The vicar's daughter, Maud, was a nice enough girl, but frankly he didn't want to go into the garden with her, and in any case she was about to disappear off to Lady Margaret Hall, which Ralph assumed was a nunnery.

Once Ralph had attained his fortieth year, he accepted that he might have to look further afield if he was to find anyone worthy of him, or at least that was until his eyes settled on Beth Trevelyan.

Ralph, as the village squire, had been invited to present the prizes at a local swimming gala, and when Beth pulled herself out of the water, he couldn't take his eyes off her. He continued to stare at the apparition as she took off her swimming cap and shook out a mass of golden curls that fell to her shoulders, completing a picture that had all the young men, and several of the older ones, looking in her direction.

Ralph was determined to add Beth to his many conquests, but as she passed by the judges' table, she didn't give him a second look. Perhaps the three-piece tweed suit, brown suede brogues, and half-hunter watch made him look a lot older than he was. He hung around outside the swimming pool hoping to speak to the goddess, but when Beth finally appeared, dressed in a simple yellow frock with a bow in her hair, she was on the arm of a fair-haired, good-looking young man who Ralph thought he recognized, but couldn't place. It didn't take Ralph long to discover that Jamie Carrigan was a tenant farmer who rented forty acres of his land and lived in one of the cottages on his estate, and that Beth was the daughter of a local publican who managed the Nethercote Arms, something else Ralph owned, but had never frequented.

What Ralph didn't know until he had made some enquiries was that the young sheep farmer had already approached Beth's father and asked for his daughter's hand in marriage. Mr Trevelyan had not only agreed to the match, but offered to hold the reception in his pub.

Despite these setbacks, Ralph assumed that once Beth knew of his interest, she wouldn't be able to resist his charms, as had been the case with several of the village girls. Not Beth, however, because when he invited her to tea at Nethercote Hall, she failed to reply. The young woman clearly didn't know her place.

As the weeks passed and several more invitations to tea, drinks and even a trip to London were refused, Ralph was at a loss to understand her attitude, not least because he wasn't in the habit of being rejected. In desperation, he resorted to suggesting a weekend in Paris, only to be turned down once again. The weeks turned into months, and nothing he came up with seemed to interest her, which only caused Ralph to become more and more obsessed with the Cornish beauty, until he could bear it no longer. He finally turned up at the Nethercote Arms unannounced and asked the publican for his daughter's hand in marriage. Mr Trevelyan was left speechless, until Ralph added a sweetener he felt confident would seal the bargain. Of course, Ralph had no intention of marrying the girl, but was determined to discover what it would be like to remove her seven veils. However, Beth was not Salome, and in any case, she already knew the man she was going to spend the rest of her life with, and it certainly wasn't Ralph Dudley Dawson Esq.

Although her father had given Jamie his blessing, neither of them had taken into consideration Beth's mother, who, like any self-respecting barmaid, knew an opportunity when she saw one. On hearing the news of the squire's interest, Mrs Trevelyan didn't waste a moment, attempting to persuade, cajole, and even bully her daughter into accepting his proposal. However, Beth continued to resist her mother's blandishments, until she discovered she was pregnant.

When Beth informed her parents who the father was, her mother was quick to point out that Jamie Carrigan was a penniless shepherd who rented forty acres of land and lived in a small cottage on the estate of a wealthy gentleman who wanted to marry her. However, Beth remained resolute in her determination to marry her lover, until the squire failed to renew the five-year lease on Jamie's forty acres, and also threatened to replace Mr Trevelyan as landlord of the Nethercote Arms, if his daughter didn't accept his proposal.

The hastily arranged marriage — Ralph couldn't wait — took place in a register office in Truro, and the reception was not held at Nethercote Hall for those in high places but at the Nethercote Arms for a select few, as Ralph didn't want his friends to realize he'd married below his station.

★ ★ ★

Mr and Mrs Dudley Dawson spent their honeymoon on the island of Rhodes, where there was little chance of them bumping into anyone they knew. When Ralph watched his wife undress for the first time, he was entranced by Beth's Botticelli figure, even more voluptuous than he'd imagined. But when they finally made love, he was disappointed by her lack of enthusiasm, and assumed it was simply because she was a shy virgin, and that given time Beth would come to enjoy his particular sexual fantasies.

Not long after the newly-weds had returned to Nethercote, Beth announced she was pregnant. Ralph wasn't surprised, after all they hadn't stopped making love during their honeymoon. Five times a night, Ralph boasted to his friends, unaware that Beth was doing no more than carrying out her mother's instructions.

Seven months later, Rupert Dudley Dawson entered the world, or at least that was the name that appeared on the birth certificate. Ralph showed no surprise at the premature birth, but did admit he was disappointed that young Rupert hadn't inherited the Dudley Dawsons' distinctive red hair and prominent nose. All in good time, he assured his friends, because like the Royal Family, Ralph would require an heir and a spare. Indeed, this mundane tale might not have advanced beyond the fate of a sad, unrequited woman and an overbearing, arrogant man, had Germany not marched into Poland on 1 September 1939.

★ ★ ★

Young Jamie Carrigan was among the first to report to the nearest recruiting office and sign up to serve his king and country with the Duke of Cornwall's Light Infantry. But then, he had lost his one true love and sought an honourable death.

Ralph, on the other hand, had no intention of joining up, and as he was over forty — just — was exempt from conscription. So while Jamie went off to fight the king's enemies, Ralph took advantage of the government's voracious appetite for more food to feed the troops, which only made him grow richer, while his marriage became impoverished.

Within a year of his betrothal, the squire's eye began to wander, and with so many of his countrymen serving on the front line his choice became even wider. He told his chums that despite Beth's unquestionable beauty, a chap needed variety. Caviar was all very well, he'd declared, but a fellow also needed the occasional dish of fish and chips.

It wasn't long before Ralph began to ignore his wife, and the only joy left in Beth's life was young Rupert, who she feared was looking more like Jamie with each passing day. Every night she would fall on her knees and pray that her former lover would survive the war and return home safely, but the only news she heard of him came from those soldiers home on leave who, whenever Jamie's name was mentioned, repeated the words brave, fearless and foolhardy.

Beth began to fear she might never see him again, but then, like so many of his comrades, he was wounded on the battlefield and sent home to recover. When she first saw Jamie limping through the village on crutches, she immediately realized what a terrible mistake she'd made, and it wasn't long before their dormant affair was rekindled.

It would be wrong to describe what took place during the next six weeks as an affair, because they fell even more deeply in love the second time around. But when Beth once again became pregnant, she realized she would have to tell her husband the truth, not least because he would know that this time it couldn't be his child.

Beth planned to tell him as soon as the doctor had confirmed she was with child, and would have done so when she returned home that afternoon, had the parlourmaid not informed her that the squire had driven into Truro for an unscheduled meeting with his solicitor.

Beth was relieved that Ralph must have somehow found out that she was pregnant, and was well prepared to face the consequences whatever wrath might be brought down on her. She sat alone in the drawing room waiting for her husband to return so she could tell him the truth. If he refused to give her a divorce, Beth had already decided she would move out of the manor house and go and live with Jamie in his little cottage. But when Ralph returned several hours later, he marched into the house, slammed the front door, and disappeared into his study without a word passing between them.

Beth sat alone for hour upon hour until she could bear it no longer, and finally summoned up the courage to face him. She left the drawing room, walked slowly across the hall and knocked quietly on his study door.

'Come,' said a terse voice. She entered the room shaking, and without even turning to face her, Ralph handed her what looked like a legal document. She read the letter twice, before she realized what had made him so angry. It was a directive from the War Office requiring him to report to his local recruitment office. The summons pointed out that the call-up age had been extended from forty-one to fifty-one, and he was therefore now eligible to join the armed forces. The only choice they gave him was the army, the navy or the air force. Beth decided this wasn't the time to let her husband know that she was pregnant.

The following day, Ralph lost his temper with the family doctor when the damn man refused to sign a certificate citing his flat feet as a reason he should be exempt from war service. But Ralph didn't give in quite that easily. He immediately wrote to the Ministry of Agriculture, pointing out the vital role he was playing in the war effort. However, an under-secretary made it clear, by return of post, that being a landowner didn't qualify him for exemption.

Undaunted, Ralph continued to search for any string he could pull to avoid being sent to the front line. He filled in applications for the Intelligence Corps — unqualified; the NAAFI — over-staffed; and the Home Guard — too young. After a month of fruitless delays, he finally accepted that he had no choice but to report to officer-training school in Berkshire. Three months later he passed out of Mons as

Second Lieutenant Ralph Dudley Dawson Esq., and was told to report back to his regimental headquarters in Truro, where he would receive his marching orders.

Beth would have enjoyed Ralph's three months' absence if Jamie hadn't fully recovered — for which she felt partly to blame — and been ordered to return to his regiment. The difference was, this time he wanted to live.

Before Jamie left, Beth wrote to her husband and told him that she would be seeking a divorce as soon as the war was over. He didn't reply.

★ ★ ★

On returning to Truro, the newly gazetted subaltern suggested to his commanding officer that his particular skills might be put to better use serving on the home front. However, as the colonel was unable to identify any such skills, Second Lieutenant Dudley Dawson was ordered to join the fifth battalion of the Duke of Cornwall's Light Infantry at Caen. That was when Ralph had his first stroke of luck. He was seconded to Command Headquarters behind Allied lines, where he quickly made himself invaluable, as he didn't intend to come face to face with the enemy if he could possibly avoid it.

During her husband's absence, Beth wrote him a second letter, fearing he might not have received the first, but once again Ralph didn't reply. He assumed the affair would quickly fizzle out, and she would surely fall in line. After all, think what she would be giving up.

Less than a mile away, serving on the front line, was Corporal Jamie Carrigan, who had just been promoted, and put in charge of his own section. As the regiment continued its advance towards the German border, Jamie was becoming more and more confident that the war was coming to an end, and it wouldn't be too long before he would return to Nethercote, marry the woman he loved and continue to farm his modest leasehold while Beth raised their children.

Unfortunately Ralph was also considering what he would do once the war was over and he had been demobbed. He'd already decided not to extend the lease on Carrigan's forty acres when it came up for its annual renewal. He would give the man thirty days' notice and tell him to vacate the cottage and seek employment elsewhere. He also intended to renege on his agreement with Mr Trevelyan to waive any future rent on the Nethercote Arms. After all, there was nothing in writing. Ralph assumed such threats would surely bring his wife to her senses, but even if she didn't fall in line, he had no intention of divorcing her.

★ ★ ★

It was after the colonel's morning meeting with his staff officers that he asked Captain Dudley Dawson to stay behind.

'Ralph,' said the commanding officer once they were alone, 'a problem has arisen that I need you to deal with discreetly. We've lost radio contact with the other battalion, and I need to urgently get a message to their commanding officer and let him know that I intend to advance at first light. Otherwise I'll be stuck here until communications are restored.'

'Understood, sir,' said Dudley Dawson.

'I can't pretend the assignment isn't risky, and wonder if you can think of anyone who might be relied on to carry out such a dangerous mission.'

'I know just the man,' said Dudley Dawson, without hesitation.

'Good, then I'll leave all the details to you. Report back to me the moment your man returns — ' he hesitated, 'or doesn't.'

Captain Dudley Dawson left the colonel's tent, jumped into his jeep and asked to be taken to the front line, which took his driver by surprise as he'd never been there before. On arrival, he immediately briefed Carrigan's section commander on the proposed mission. The young lieutenant was surprised by the colonel's choice of runner, remembering that the regiment's cross-country champion was also in his platoon, but he wasn't in the habit of questioning his commanding officer's orders.

Ralph watched from a distance as Lieutenant Jackson briefed Carrigan on the importance of the assignment. A few minutes later, the corporal climbed out of the trench, and without looking back set off across no-man's-land.

'How long do you think it will take him to reach the other battalion?' asked Ralph after Jackson reported back to him.

'If he makes it, sir, an hour at the most. But then he still has to get back.'

73

'Let's hope he does,' said Ralph in his most sincere voice.

Lieutenant Jackson nodded and said, 'God help the man.'

Ralph didn't believe in God, but decided he would hang around for a couple of hours or so before he reported back to the colonel that sadly Carrigan had not returned, and therefore the mission would have to be aborted.

An hour passed and there was no sign of Carrigan. Another fifteen minutes, still no sign. But Ralph remained huddled in a corner of the trench for another half hour before he allowed himself the suggestion of a smile.

'Damned fine effort,' he said to Lieutenant Jackson, who was peering through a pair of binoculars across the wooded landscape. 'One couldn't have asked more of Carrigan,' continued Ralph as he checked his watch. 'Well, I'd better get back to HQ and let the colonel know that the advance will have to be delayed until we can make radio contact. Damn fine effort,' he repeated. 'I'll be recommending to the colonel that Carrigan is awarded the Military Medal for service above and beyond the call of duty. It's the least he deserves,' he added before he began to crawl along the trench.

'Hang on, sir,' said Lieutenant Jackson. 'I think I can see someone in the distance.'

Ralph crawled back, fearing the worst. 'He's about a hundred yards away,' added Jackson, 'and heading straight for us.'

'Where?' said Ralph, leaping up and staring across the barren terrain.

'Get down, sir,' shouted the lieutenant, but he was too late, because the bullet hit Captain Ralph Dudley Dawson Esq. in the forehead, and he sank back down into the mud just as Carrigan dived into the trench.

★ ★ ★

The Duke of Cornwall's Light Infantry continued their advance towards Berlin at first light, while a coffin containing the body of Captain Dudley Dawson was shipped back to England, along with a letter of condolence from his commanding officer. The colonel was able to assure the grieving widow that her husband had sacrificed his life while serving his country on the front line.

The fifth battalion of the Duke of Cornwall's Light Infantry won a great battle that day, and a year later at a service held in Truro Cathedral, the name of Normandy was added to the regimental colours.

Among those seated in the congregation was Corporal Jamie Carrigan MM, along with his wife and two children, Rupert and Susie. Unfortunately, Ralph Dudley Dawson Esq. hadn't considered the possibility of mortality, and died intestate. His wife, being the next of kin, inherited a thousand-acre estate, ten thousand sheep, Nethercote Hall and all his other worldly goods.

Jamie Carrigan never thought of himself as the local squire, just a farm manager who'd been lucky enough to marry the only woman he'd ever loved.

THE CAR PARK ATTENDANT

It would never have happened if his uncle Bert hadn't taken him to the zoo.

Joe Simpson wanted to play football for Manchester United, and when he was selected to captain Barnsford Secondary Modern, he was confident it could only be a matter of time before United's chief scout would be standing on the touchline demanding to know his name. But by the time Joe walked onto the pitch for the last match of the season, not even the Barnsford Rovers coach had bothered to come and watch him, so with only one GCE (maths), he was at a bit of a loss to know what he was going to do for the rest of his life.

'You could always join Dad as a council car park attendant,' suggested his mum. 'At least the pay's steady.'

'You must be joking,' said Joe.

It only took a month and seven job interviews for Joe to discover it was the council car park, or stacking shelves at the local supermarket. Joe was just about to sign on the dole and join what his dad called 'the great unwashed' when he was offered a job at the Co-op.

Joe lasted ten days as a shelf stacker before he was shown the door, and he had to admit to his mum that perhaps it hadn't helped when he put two hundred cans of Whiskas next to the prime cuts of beef.

'A vacancy's come up at Lakeside Drive car park,' his father told him, 'and if you want, lad, I could have a word with boss.'

'I'll do it for a couple of weeks,' said Joe, 'while I look for a real job.'

Joe wouldn't admit to his father that he rather enjoyed being a car park attendant. He was out in the open air, meeting people and chatting to customers while working out how much to charge them once they'd told him how long they wanted to park; something his dad had never got the hang of, but then he hadn't got a GCE in maths.

Joe quickly got to know several of the regulars, and the cars they drove. His favourite was Mr Mason, who turned up in a different vehicle every day, which puzzled Joe, until his dad told him he was a second-hand car dealer, and he probably liked to know what he was selling.

'Your dad's right,' Mr Mason told him. 'But it's even more important to know what you're buying. Why don't you come over to the showroom sometime, and I'll show you what I mean?'

The next time Joe had a day off, he decided to take up Mr Mason's offer and visit the car showroom. It was love at first sight when he saw the Jaguar XK120 in racing green, and second sight when he saw the boss's book-keeper in dashing red, but neither was available for a council car park attendant. Not least because Molly Stokes had seven GCEs and had also taken a bookkeeping course at Barnsford Polytechnic.

From that day on, Joe found any excuse to visit Mr Mason, not to see the latest models, but to talk to the first girl he didn't think was soppy. Molly finally gave in and agreed to go to the cinema with him to see John Wayne in *The Quiet Man*, not Molly's first choice. The following week they went to see Spencer Tracy in *Pat and Mike*, her choice, and Joe accepted that was how it was going to be for the rest of their lives.

* * *

A year later, Joe proposed to Molly on bended knee, and even bought an engagement ring from H. Samuel, which he'd spent two weeks' salary on. But she turned him down. Not because she didn't want to marry Joe, but she wouldn't consider marriage until they could afford a place of their own.

'But if we get married,' said Joe, 'we can put our name down for a council house, and not have to go on living with my parents.' Molly didn't want to live in a council house.

And then the worst thing that could happen, happened. Joe got the sack.

'It ain't that you're no good at the job, lad,' said the supervisor, 'but bosses at council want cutbacks, so it's last in, first out, and as you've only been with us for a couple of years, I'll have to let you go. Sorry about that.'

Just when Joe thought it couldn't get any worse, Molly announced she was pregnant.

They were married a month later, his dad having told him in no uncertain terms, 'There's never been a bastard in our family, and we won't be startin' now.'

Once the banns had been read, the wedding was held three weeks later at St Mary the Immaculate parish church, with a reception afterwards at the King's Arms across the road. No expense spared. The girls drank Babycham, while the lads downed pints of Barnsford bitter and cleared the pub out of crisps and pork pies. Everyone had a good time. But when the newly married couple woke up in Mr Simpson's spare room the following morning, Joe was still on the dole, and Molly was still pregnant, and they didn't have enough money for a honeymoon, even a weekend in Blackpool.

That was when their uncle Bert, without intending to, changed their whole lives.

Uncle Bert worked at Barnsford Zoo, where he cleaned out Big Boris's cage, the lion folks came to see from all over the county. It was at his wedding bash over a pint of bitter that Bert told Joe a job might be coming up at the zoo, and if he popped in on Monday, he'd introduce him to the manager, Mr Turner.

On Monday morning, Joe put on a clean shirt and a pair of neatly pressed trousers, and borrowed one of his father's two ties. He was on the top deck of a double-decker bus on his way to the zoo, when he first spotted the piece of land in the distance. He couldn't take his eyes off it. When he got off the bus, he didn't head straight for the nearest turnstile, but walked in the opposite direction.

Joe stood and stared at a large plot of waste

land that must have had a hundred vehicles parked on it. He spent the day watching as cars, vans, even coaches came and went, filling any space that was available with no rhyme or reason, some of the drivers not even visiting the zoo. An idea was beginning to form in his mind, and by the end of the day, Joe's only thought was, could he get away with it?

'So did Mr Turner offer you the job?' asked Molly when Joe arrived back just in time for tea.

'I never saw Mr Turner,' Joe admitted. 'Something came up.'

'What came up?' demanded Molly.

Joe buttoned his lip when his dad strolled in, and it wasn't until they climbed into bed later that night that he told Molly how he'd spent his day, and then shared his big idea with her.

'You're daft as a pumpkin, Joe Simpson. That's council land, and you'd be done for trespassing, and what's more I'll prove it, then you won't have to waste any more time and can go and get that job at the zoo before someone else grabs it.'

Molly spent the following morning at Barnsford Town Hall, where she visited the estates department, and got chatting to a young man who, after checking several ordnance survey maps, couldn't be sure who did own the land, the council or the zoo. Molly still wasn't convinced. But at least she now considered it a risk worth taking.

Joe took the bus to the zoo every day for the next week, where he made notes of how many people parked on the land, and roughly how long they spent visiting the zoo. He waited until they closed for the night and the last car had departed, before he paced out the boundaries. He wrote in his little book: 226 paces by 172.

The following day, he returned to his old stomping ground on Lakeside Drive, explaining that he needed a word with his old man. But once he got there, he measured a council parking space, this time not in paces, but in feet with an old school ruler: 18ft by 9ft for cars and vans, 40ft by 11ft for coaches. His dad couldn't make head nor tail of what the lad was up to.

Joe spent the weekend trying to calculate how many cars could be parked on the zoo site. After he double-checked his figures, he decided there was enough room for 114 cars and five coaches. When Molly returned from work that night, he showed her his planned layout for the car park. She was impressed, but remained sceptical.

'You'll never get away with it!' she said.

'Maybe not, but as no one else is offering me a job, I've got nothing to lose.'

Molly raised an eyebrow. 'So what are you going to do next?'

'I'm going to learn how to paint a parking space in the dark.'

'Then you'll need a torch, and a pot of white emulsion,' said Molly, 'not to mention a brush, a bucket of water, and a broom to clear the space, as well as some string and nails to mark out a straight line even before you can start thinking about painting anything. And by the way, Joe, while you're at it, I'd recommend you start by trying to paint four straight lines in the light.'

'I thought you didn't believe in my plan?' said Joe.

'I don't, but if you're going to give it a go, at least do the job properly.'

Joe visited every paint merchant in the town, while Molly went off to work at Mason's. After a day of comparing prices, Joe came to the conclusion he could only afford to buy six tins of white paint if he was still going to have enough money left over to get all the other bits and pieces Molly had insisted on.

'I can get the string, nails, a hammer and a large broom from Mason's,' said Molly when she arrived home after work that evening. 'So you can cross them off your list.'

'But what about the bucket?'

'Well, borrow Mr Mason's fire bucket, and then you can fill it up in the public toilet outside the zoo.' Joe nodded. 'Next thing you'll have to do is a dry run,' said Molly.

'A dry run?'

'Yes, you'll need to find a derelict council site and practise painting one space, until you've got the hang of it.'

When Molly went to work the next day, Joe headed off to an old bomb site on the outskirts of town, and painted his first car parking space. Not as easy as he had thought it would be. However, by the end of the week, he could complete one in forty minutes that wasn't half bad. The only problem was that he ran out of paint, and although he had nearly perfected his technique, Molly had to sacrifice a week's wages so he could replenish his stocks. By early

December, he was ready to move onto the site.

'Our next problem,' said Molly, 'is finding a time when you can paint the parking spots while no one else is around to see what you're up to.'

'I've already worked that one out,' said Joe. 'This year Christmas Day falls on a Friday, so no one will be visiting the site on the Friday, Saturday or Sunday, and even bank holiday Monday, when the zoo will still be closed. So I could probably paint a hundred spaces in that time.'

'I think a dozen would be quite enough to start with,' said Molly. 'Let's make sure your big idea works before we spend any more money than necessary. Don't forget that Mr Mason started his business with six cars, and now he's got a showroom with over a hundred in the forecourt, as well as a Jaguar dealership.'

Joe reluctantly agreed, and began to prepare himself for the big day.

★ ★ ★

Joe couldn't get to sleep on Christmas Eve, and was up the following morning even before Molly had woken. He put on a T-shirt, a pair of jeans, a sweater, and his old school gym shoes. He crept downstairs and collected an ancient pram from the shed at the bottom of the garden, which Molly had filled the night before with everything he would need.

He pushed the pram all the way to the zoo, and spent the next few hours sweeping the ground and clearing it of leaves, dirt and dust.

Once he was satisfied that the site had been properly prepared, he measured out his first parking space with the help of a tape measure borrowed from his mum's sewing basket. He then knocked nails into the four corners, to which he attached a length of string. He stood back and admired the canvas on which the artist was about to work.

It was just after ten by the time Joe had completed his first parking space, and he was exhausted. He hid the pram in a clump of trees, and somehow still found enough energy to run all the way home. He arrived back even before his father had got up, and only his mother asked how he got white paint on his jeans.

'My fault,' said Molly, without explanation.

After Christmas lunch, Joe waited for everyone to settle in front of the television, or fall asleep, before he once again set off for the zoo. By the time the street lights came on at four o'clock, he'd completed two more spaces. On Boxing Day, another four, and by five o'clock on 27 December all twelve spaces were finished and ready for occupation. He hoped they'd all be dry by the time he returned the following morning.

★ ★ ★

Barnsford Zoo opened its doors to the public at ten o'clock on Tuesday morning, but business was slow. Joe stood on the corner of the site and watched at a distance. Whenever a car appeared, it immediately drove into one of his neatly painted spaces, now dry, which at least gave him a degree of confidence. He carried out the same routine for the next three days, and discovered the pattern didn't vary. But then, the British are a nation who believe in queues, and behaving in an orderly fashion.

On 31 December and 1 and 2 January, Joe went back to work, and he and Molly celebrated the New Year having painted twenty parking spaces.

'Quite enough,' declared Molly, 'because you've still got to find out if the public will wear it.'

★ ★ ★

Joe rose at six o'clock the next morning, put on his old council parking attendant's uniform, and collected one of his father's discarded ticket collecting machines from the shed.

He took a bus to the site, and was standing on the parking lot long before the zoo opened for business. He patrolled his twenty spaces like a lion protecting its cubs, and when his first potential customer appeared, he walked tentatively over to a man who had parked in one of the spaces.

'Good morning, sir,' said Joe. 'That will be two shillings.' If the man had told him to bugger off, he would have done just that, but he meekly handed over a florin.

'Thank you, sir,' said Joe, issuing him with a ticket before touching his peaked cap. His first customer.

By the end of the day, he'd had fourteen

customers, and collected one pound and eight shillings. By the end of the first week, he'd pocketed £31, and took Molly out for a drink at the pub, where they shared a Scotch egg.

Joe wanted to splash out and go to the Swan, where you could get a three-course meal and a half bottle of wine for £3, but Molly wouldn't hear of it, saying, 'It will only make folks suspicious, and give the game away.' She even introduced him to the words 'cash flow'.

On the Monday, when the zoo was closed, Joe could have taken a day off, but instead, he laboured away, painting another six spaces, and as each day passed, the rectangles increased along with his income, causing him to grow more and more confident. However, it was on the Tuesday of the third week that he saw Mr Turner, the zoo manager, heading towards him and assumed the game was up.

'Morning, Mr . . . ?'

'Joe,' he said.

'Could we have a private word, Joe?'

'Yes, of course, Mr Turner.'

'When I've parked here in the past,' said the zoo manager, 'I've never had to pay.'

'And you won't have to in the future, Mr Turner,' said Joe.

'But now the council's taken over the site, surely I'll be expected — '

'You won't be expected to pay a penny, Mr Turner. In fact I'm going to allocate you your own private space that no one else will be able to park in.'

'Won't the council kick up a fuss?'

'I won't say anything if you don't,' said Joe, touching his nose.

'That's good of you, Joe,' said Turner. 'Let me know if I can ever do anything for you.'

Joe selected the space directly opposite the entrance to the zoo and spent the rest of the day carefully painting the words ZOO MANAGER ONLY.

★　★　★

When Molly left her job at Mason's to have the baby, Joe suggested she handle the cash and keep the books.

Molly also opened a bank account with Barclays, and paid in just over £20 a week, the average wage for a council parking attendant, and placed the rest of the cash under a floorboard in their bedroom.

Although Molly kept the books in apple pie order, even she had to take some time off when Joe Junior was born. His birth only gave the proud father the incentive to paint even more spaces, and within a year, all 119 slots were in place, with a special area reserved for coaches.

When the time came for Molly to return to work, she didn't go back to Mason's, but joined Joe officially as his bookkeeper and secretary. She paid herself £25 a week. However, it didn't help the cash flow problem, as they had to take up more and more floorboards, but she was already working on how to deal with that particular problem.

★ ★ ★

It was Molly who suggested that the time had come for them to take a trip to Macclesfield.

'Macclesfield wouldn't be my first choice for a holiday,' said Joe.

'We're not going on holiday,' said Molly, 'just a day trip. If you look at your father's latest ticket machine, you'll see who the manufacturer is, and I think it's time we paid them a visit.'

As the zoo was always closed on a Monday, Molly borrowed a van from Mr Mason and the three of them set off for Macclesfield. The showroom turned out to be a treasure trove of uniforms, machines and all the other accessories any self-respecting car park attendant needed to do his job. Joe ended up acquiring two outfits (summer and winter) with ZOO printed on the shoulder, the latest collecting machine, a peaked cap, and a small enamel badge that announced SUPERVISOR, which he couldn't resist, although Molly wasn't at all sure about it. Her only acquisitions were a large bookkeeper's ledger and a filing cabinet.

It was on the way back to Barnsford that Molly dropped two bombshells. 'I'm pregnant again,' she said, 'but at least the council have finally offered us a house.'

'But I thought you didn't want to live in a council house, and in any case we've got enough cash to put down a deposit on a bungalow on the Woolwich estate,' said Joe.

'Can't risk it,' said Molly. 'If we did that, folks might start gossiping and wonder how you

91

earned that sort of money as a car park attendant, and don't forget, most people think I'm still out of work.'

'But what's the point of making all this money, if we can't enjoy it?' demanded Joe.

'Don't worry yourself. I have plans for that too.'

★   ★   ★

Six months later, Mr and Mrs Simpson, Joe Jr and Janet moved into their council house on the Keir Hardie estate. While folks might have thought their new neighbours were living in a council house, if they'd ever been invited inside they would have discovered the Simpsons weren't doing their shopping at the Co-op, but then they never were invited inside.

And as well as tufted carpets, a space age kitchen, a large-screen TV, and a three-piece suite that wasn't bought on the never-never, they still had a cash flow problem. But Joe felt confident Molly would come up with a solution.

'We won't be going to Blackpool for our summer holiday this year,' she announced over breakfast one morning.

'Then where are we going, Mum?' demanded Joe Jr.

'Don't speak with your mouth full,' said Molly. 'We're going to Majorca.'

Joe wanted to ask 'Where's that?', but was rescued by Janet, who asked the same question.

'It's an island in the Mediterranean, which not many people from Barnsford will have heard of, and are even more unlikely to visit,' which seemed to silence all three of them.

Joe and Molly always took their holiday in the zoo's quietest fortnight of the year, and as the day approached, the children became more and more excited, because it would be their first trip on a plane. Joe's and Molly's too, come to that, but they didn't mention it.

To do Joe justice, it was his idea to employ a bright university student, preferably an immigrant, to cover for him whenever he was away on holiday. He always paid the lad in cash, and although he didn't make much of a profit during that fortnight, the regulars were kept happy, and there were never any questions about why the car park wasn't manned.

'And if anyone asks where I am,' said Joe, 'just tell them I'm on holiday with the family in Blackpool.'

Once the family arrived in Majorca, Molly didn't waste any time. While Joe took the children to the beach, she visited every estate agent in Palma. When they got back on the plane a fortnight later, Joe had put on half a stone, the children were nut brown, and Molly had put down a deposit on a front-line plot in Puerto de Pollença, overlooking the sea.

The estate agent made no comment when she signed the contract and handed over the £5,000 deposit in cash. By the time they'd visited Majorca six times, the land belonged to them.

Molly then set about looking for a local architect. She chose a German, much to Joe's disapproval, who also didn't raise an eyebrow when his quarterly payments were made in cash.

A year later, a JCB rolled onto the site, and the builder licked his lips when rolls of twenty-pound notes changed hands on a regular basis, even if the project manager found Molly a bit of a handful.

So while Joe and Molly continued to live a frugal existence in Barnsford, with Joe's only extravagance a season ticket for Barnsford Rovers, who still languished in the bottom half of the third division, Molly did allow herself the occasional visit to The Smoke to see the latest musical and have an Indian curry at Veeraswamy. But they always travelled back to Barnsford second class in case anyone spotted them. However, during the summer holidays, the family could always be found residing in their luxury villa overlooking the sea in the Bay of Pollença.

★　★　★

When Joe's father retired at the age of sixty, Joe sent his mum and dad for a cruise on the *QE2*, explaining that they'd had a little win on the Premium Bonds. And two years later, when the zoo had an appeal for a new elephant house, the manager (Joe's fifth) was delighted when they received an anonymous donation of £10,000, but was just a little surprised that it arrived in a large brown paper bag.

Joe was particularly proud when Joe Jr was offered a place at Leeds University to study law, another first for the Simpson family, but Janet

94

trumped her brother two years later when she won a scholarship to read English at Durham.

'What are we going to do when the time comes for us to retire?' asked Joe, aware that Molly would have already given the problem some considerable thought.

'We'll go and live in Majorca and, to quote the good Lord, enjoy the fruits of our labour.'

'But what about my car park?'

'You can leave someone else to worry about that.'

★ ★ ★

Being a conventional sort of chap, Joe also retired on his sixtieth birthday, and after handing back the keys of their council house, he and Molly packed up everything they needed (very little), and headed for the airport with two one-way tickets.

It wasn't long before Joe became a vice president of Real Mallorca, who were at least in the top half of the second division, and deputy chairman of the local Rotary club, while Molly became honorary treasurer of the residents' association.

Joe Jr was now a practising barrister on the northern circuit, while Janet taught English at Roundhay grammar school. They both paid regular visits to their parents in Majorca, accompanied by Charlie, Rachel and Joe very Jr, who Joe and Molly adored.

★ ★ ★

'Have you seen what they've done with my car park?' said Joe one evening, after reading his weekly copy of the *Yorkshire Post*. 'Daft pillocks,' he said as he continued to read the article.

On 2 January, the new manager of the zoo, a Mr Braithwaite, called the estates department at Barnsford City Council, to ask when Joe Simpson's replacement would be reporting for work.

'Who's Joe Simpson?' the estates manager asked.

'He's the man who ran the car park opposite the zoo. Has done for the past forty years. We even gave him a farewell party.'

'I don't know what you're talking about,' said the estates manager, 'I always assumed you owned the land.'

'But we thought you did!' said Braithwaite.

'Daft pillocks,' repeated Joe as he put down his paper and joined Molly in the kitchen. 'If manager 'ad bin half awake, he'd 'ave kept his mouth shut, and only the zoo would have benefited,' he told his wife, 'which is what I'd always wanted. But no, he had to consult council chairman, Alderman Appleyard, who thought they should take legal advice, which has ended up with a lengthy court battle between Barnsford City Council and the zoo. Result? Both sides lost out, while weeds are sprouting up all over my car park.'

Three years later a judge finally ruled that the council should take charge of the car park, but any profits were to be divided equally between the two. A typical British compromise, where only the lawyers benefit, was Joe's opinion when he read the latest news coming out of Yorkshire.

'I'm only surprised,' said Molly, 'that they've not come after us.'

'No chance,' said Joe. 'I reckon that'd make council look like a bunch of wallies. No, least said, soonest mended. And you can be of one thing, no one will stand up and take responsibility. Don't forget, that lot will be coming up for re-election in May, so mum's the word.'

★　★　★

When I last had dinner with Joe and Molly in Pollença, I couldn't resist asking him how much he thought he'd made over the years, as a car park attendant.

'Supervisor,' he corrected me, not answering my question.

'Three million, four hundred and twenty-two thousand, three hundred and nineteen pounds,' replied Molly.

'That sounds 'bout right,' said Joe, 'but next time you're in Barnsford, Jeff lad, take a look at zoo's new aquarium. Summat the missus and I are right chuffed about!'

★　★　★

Joe and Molly Simpson are buried next to each other in the churchyard of St Mary the Immaculate in Barnsford. Something else Molly insisted on.

A WASTED HOUR

Kelley always thumbed a ride back to college, but never told her parents. She knew they wouldn't approve.

Her father would drive her to the station on the first day of term, when she would hang around on the platform until she was certain he was on his way back home. She would then walk the couple of miles to the freeway.

There were two good reasons why Kelley preferred to thumb a ride back to Stanford rather than take a bus or train. Twelve round trips a year meant she could save over a hundred dollars, which her father could ill afford after being laid off by the water company. In any case he and Ma had already made quite enough sacrifices to ensure she could attend college, without causing them any further expense.

But Kelley's second reason for preferring to thumb rides was that when she graduated she wanted to be a writer, and during the past three years she'd met some fascinating people on the short journey from Salinas to Palo Alto, who were often willing to share their experiences with a stranger they were unlikely to meet again.

One fellow had worked as a messenger on Wall Street during the Depression, while another had won the Silver Star at Monte Cassino, but her favourite was the man who'd spent a day fishing with President Roosevelt.

Kelley also had golden rules about who she wouldn't accept a ride from. Truck drivers were top of the list as they only ever had one thing on their mind. The next were vehicles with two or three young men on board. In fact she avoided most drivers under the age of sixty, especially those behind the wheel of a sports car.

The first car to slow down had two young fellows in it, and if that wasn't warning enough, the empty beer cans on the back seat certainly were. They looked disappointed when she firmly shook her head, and after a few raucous catcalls continued on their way.

The next vehicle to pull over was a truck, but she didn't even look up at the driver, just continued walking. He eventually drove off, honking his horn in disgust.

The third was a pick-up truck, with a couple in the front who looked promising, until she saw a German shepherd lounging across the back seat that looked as if he hadn't been fed in a while. Kelley politely told them she was allergic to dogs — well, except for Daisy, her cocker spaniel back home, whom she adored.

And then she spotted a pre-war Studebaker slowly ambling along towards her. Kelley faced the oncoming car, smiled, and raised her thumb. The car slowed, and pulled off the road. She walked quickly up to the passenger door to see an elderly gentleman leaning across and winding down the window.

'Where are you headed, young lady?' he asked.

'Stanford, sir,' she replied.

'I'll be driving past the front gates, so jump in.'

Kelley didn't hesitate, because he met all of her most stringent requirements: over sixty, wearing a wedding ring, well-spoken and polite. When she got in, Kelley sank back into the leather seat, her only worry being whether either the car or the old man would make it.

While he looked to his left and concentrated on getting back onto the road, she took a closer look at him. He had mousy grey hair, a sallow, lined complexion, like well-worn leather, and the only thing she didn't like was the cigarette dangling from the corner of his mouth. He wore an open-neck checked shirt, and a corduroy jacket with leather patches on the elbows.

Her supervisor had told her on numerous occasions that if she wanted to be a writer she would have to get some experience of life, especially other people's lives, and although her driver didn't look an obvious candidate to expand her horizons, there was only one way she was going to find out.

'Thanks for stopping,' she said. 'My name's Kelley.'

'John,' he replied, taking one hand off the wheel to shake hands with her. The rough hands of a farm labourer, was her first thought. 'What are you majoring in, Kelley?' he asked.

'Modern American literature.'

'There hasn't been much of that lately,' he suggested. 'But then times are a changin'. When I was at Stanford, there were no women on the campus, even at night.'

Kelley was surprised that John had been to Stanford. 'What degree did you take, sir?'

'John,' he insisted. 'It's bad enough being old, without being reminded of the fact by a young woman.' She laughed. 'I studied English literature, like you. Mark Twain, Herman Melville, James Thurber, Longfellow, but I'm afraid I flunked out. Never took my degree, which I still bitterly regret.'

Kelley gave him another look and wondered if the car would ever move out of third gear. She was just about to ask why he flunked out, when he said, 'And who are now considered to be the modern giants of American literature, dare I ask?'

'Hemingway, Steinbeck, Bellow and Faulkner,' she replied.

'Do you have a favourite?' he asked, his eyes never leaving the road ahead.

'Yes I do. I read *The Grapes of Wrath* when I was twelve years old, and I consider it to be one of the great novels of the twentieth century. '*And the little screaming fact that sounds through all history: repression works only to strengthen and knit the repressed.*''

'I'm impressed,' he said. 'Although my favourite will always be *Of Mice and Men*.'

'*'Guy don't need no sense to be a nice fella,'* said Kelley. '*'Seems to me sometimes it jus' works the other way around. Take a real smart guy and he ain't hardly ever a nice fella.*''

'I don't think you'll be flunking your exams,' said John with a chuckle, which gave Kelley the opportunity to begin her interrogation.

'So what did you do after you left Stanford?'

'My father wanted me to work on his farm

back in Monterey, which I managed for a couple of years, but it just wasn't me, so I rebelled and got a job as a tour guide at Lake Tahoe.'

'That must have been fun.'

'Sure was. Lots of dames, but the pay was lousy. So my friend Ed and I decided to travel up and down the California coast collecting biological specimens, but that didn't turn out to be very lucrative either.'

'Did you try and look for something more permanent after that?' asked Kelley.

'No, can't pretend I did. Well, at least not until war broke out, when I got a job as a war correspondent on the *Herald Tribune*.'

'Wow, that must have been exciting,' said Kelley. 'Right there among the action, and then reporting everything you'd seen to the folks back home.'

'That was the problem. I got too close to the action and ended up with a whole barrel of shotgun up my backside, and had to be shipped back to the States. So I lost my job at the *Trib*, along with my first wife.'

'Your first wife?'

'Did I forget to mention Carol?' he said. 'She lasted thirteen years before she was replaced by Gwyn, who only managed five. But to do her justice, which is quite difficult, she gave me two great sons.'

'So what happened once you'd fully recovered from your wounds?'

'I began working with some of the immigrants who were flooding into California after the war. I'm from German stock myself, so I knew what they were going through, and felt a lot of sympathy for them.'

'Is that what you've been doing ever since?'

'No, no. When Johnson decided to invade Vietnam, the *Trib* offered me my old job back. Seems they couldn't find too many people who considered being shipped off to 'Nam a good career move.'

Kelley laughed. 'But at least this time you survived.'

'Well, I would have done if the CIA hadn't asked me to work for them at the same time.'

'Am I allowed to ask what you did for them?' she said, looking more closely at the old man.

'Wrote one version of what was going on in 'Nam for the *Trib*, while letting the CIA know what was really happening. But then I had an advantage over my colleagues that only the CIA knew about.'

Kelley would have asked how come, but John answered her question before she could speak.

'Both my sons, John Jr and Thomas, were serving in the front line, so I was getting information my fellow hacks weren't.'

'The *Trib* must have loved that.'

'I'm afraid not,' said John. 'The editor sacked me the minute he found out I was workin' for the CIA. Said I'd forfeited my journalistic integrity and gone native, not to mention the fact I was being paid by two masters.'

Kelley was spellbound.

'And to be fair,' he continued, 'I couldn't disagree with them. And in any case, I was gettin' more and more disillusioned by what was happening in 'Nam, and even began to question whether we still occupied the moral high ground.'

'So what did you do when you got back home this time?' asked Kelley, who was beginning to consider the trip was every bit as exciting as the journey she'd experienced with the fellow who'd spent a day fishing with President Roosevelt.

'When I got home,' John continued, 'I discovered my second wife had shacked up with some other fella. Can't say I blame her. Not that I was single for too long, because soon after I married Elaine. I can only tell you one thing I know for sure, Kelley, three wives is more than enough for any man.'

'So what did you do next?' asked Kelley, aware it wouldn't be too long before they reached the university campus.

'Elaine and I went down South, where I wrote about the Civil Rights movement for any rag that was willing to print my views. But unfortunately I got myself into trouble again when I locked horns with J. Edgar Hoover and refused to cooperate with the FBI, and tell them what I'd found out following my meetings with Martin Luther King Jr and Ralph Abernathy. In fact Hoover got so angry, he tried to label me a communist. But this time he couldn't make it stick, so he amused himself by having the IRS audit me every year.'

'You met Martin Luther King Jr and Ralph Abernathy?'

'Sure did. And John Kennedy come to that, God rest his soul.'

On hearing that he'd actually met JFK, Kelley suddenly had so many more questions she wanted to ask, but she could now see the university's Hoover Tower becoming larger by the minute.

'What an amazing life you've led,' said Kelley, who was disappointed the journey was coming to an end.

'I fear I may have made it sound more exciting than it really was,' said John. 'But then an old man's reminiscences cannot always be relied on. So, Kelley, what are you going to do with your life?'

'I want to be a writer,' she told him. 'My dream is that in fifty years' time, students studying modern American literature at Stanford will include the name of Kelley Ragland.'

'Nothing wrong with that,' said John. 'But if you'll allow an old man to give you a piece of advice, don't be in too much of a hurry to write the Great American Novel. Get as much experience of the world and people as you can before you sit down and put pen to paper,' he added as he brought the car to a stuttering halt outside the college gates. 'I can promise you, Kelley, you won't regret it.'

'Thank you for the lift, John,' said Kelley, as she got out of the car. She walked quickly round to the driver's side to say goodbye to the old man as he wound down the window. 'It's been fascinating to hear all about your life.'

'I enjoyed talking to you too,' said John, 'and can only hope I live long enough to read your first novel, especially as you were kind enough to say how much you'd enjoyed my work, which, if I remember, you first read when you were only twelve years old.'

THE ROAD TO DAMASCUS

Do you, like me, sometimes wonder what happened to your school contemporaries when they left and went out into the real world, particularly those in the year above you, whose names you could never forget? While those who followed in the forms below, you would rarely remember.

Take Nick Atkins, for example, who was captain of cricket. I assumed he would captain Yorkshire and England, but in fact after a couple of outings for the county Second XI, he ended up as a regional manager for the Halifax Building Society. And then there was Stuart Baggaley, who told everyone he was going to be the Member of Parliament for Leeds Central, and twenty years later reached the dizzy heights of chairman of Ways and Means on the Huddersfield District Council. And last, and certainly least, was Derek Mott, who trained to be an actuary, and when I last heard, was running an amusement arcade in Blackpool.

However, it was clear to me even then that one boy was certain to fulfil his ambition, not least because his destiny had been decided while he was still in the womb. After all, Mark Bairstow was the son of Sir Ernest Bairstow, the chairman of Bairstow & Son, the biggest iron foundry in Yorkshire, and therefore in the world.

I never got to know Bairstow while we were at

school: not only because he was in the year above me, but because he was literally in a different class. While most boys walked, cycled or took the bus to school, Bairstow arrived each morning in a chauffeur-driven limousine. His father couldn't spare the time to drive his son to school, it was explained, because he was already at the foundry, and his mother couldn't drive.

I really didn't mind the fact that his school uniform was so much smarter than mine, and that his shoes were handmade escaped me altogether. However, I was aware that he was taller and better-looking than me, and clearly brighter, because he was offered a place at Gonville and Caius College, Cambridge (pronounced Keys — something else I didn't know at the time), to read modern languages.

I actually spoke to Bairstow for the first time when I entered the lower sixth, and he had been appointed school captain, but then only because I was a library monitor and had to report to him once a month. And indeed, if we hadn't gone on holiday together — well, I shouldn't exaggerate . . .

Fred Costello, the senior history master, was organizing one of his annual school excursions to the Continent, as it was known before it became the Common Market, or the EEC, and as I was studying history and hoping to go to university, my parents thought it might be wise for me to sign up for the trip to Germany.

When we all clambered on board the train at Leeds Central to set out on the journey, I was surprised to see Mark Bairstow was among our party. Well not quite, because he sat in a first-class carriage with Clive Dangerfield, who was also going up to Cambridge, so we didn't see them again until we all pitched up at our little hotel in Berlin. I shared a room with my best friend Ben Levy, while Bairstow and Dangerfield occupied a suite on the top floor.

There were fifteen of us in the party, and I spent most of my time with Ben who, like me, supported Leeds United, Yorkshire and England, in that order. It was our first trip abroad and therefore one we weren't likely to forget.

Mr Costello was an enlightened schoolmaster who had served as a lieutenant in the Second World War and seen action at El Alamein, but believed passionately that Britain should join the Common Market, if for no other reason than it would ensure there wouldn't be a third world war.

My abiding memory of Berlin was not the Opera House, or even the Brandenburg Gate, but a concrete monstrosity that stretched like a poisonous snake across the centre of a once united city.

'I want you to imagine,' said Mr Costello, as we stared up at the Wall, 'a twelve-foot barrier being built from the Mersey to the Humber, and you never being able to visit any of your family or friends who live on the other side.'

The thought had never crossed my mind.

After a few days in Berlin, we boarded a charabanc for Dresden, but never once left the coach as we stared out of the windows in disbelief to see what was left of that once historic city. It made me feel that perhaps at times the British had also behaved like barbarians. I was pleased when the coach turned round and headed back to Berlin.

The following day was a schoolboy's dream. After driving to Regensburg, we spent the morning on a coal barge trudging sedately up the Danube, billowing black smoke as we made our way to Passau. After lunch, we took a train to Munich, where we spent three days in a youth hostel with young women actually sleeping in dorms on the floor below us. The next morning we explored the capital of Bavaria, and there wasn't much sign that this had once been the birthplace of the Nazi party. I much admired the Residenz, the vast palace of the Wittelsbachs, where Mark Bairstow looked so relaxed he might have been visiting an old friend at home.

In the evening, we went to the Cuvilliés-Theater to see *La Bohème*, my first introduction to opera, which was to become a lifelong passion. It would be years before I appreciated how much I owed to Mr Costello, a teacher whose lessons stretched far beyond the classroom.

The following day, we visited the Alte Pinakothek, and I can't pretend I was able to fully appreciate Dürer or Cranach, as I couldn't take my eyes off a group of girls who were being shown around the gallery by the same guide. One in particular caught my attention.

My extra-curricular activities in Bavaria included my first experience of beer, frankfurters, attending the opera, and being kissed goodnight by a girl, although I don't think she was overwhelmed. I just wished we'd had another week as she was clearly in the class above me.

On our final day, Mr Costello brought us all back down to earth when we boarded a bus that didn't announce its destination on the front. We must have travelled some fourteen miles north of Munich before we reached a small town called Dachau. Of course, I knew my closest friend was Jewish, but I only thought of him as a classmate, and we never quarrelled about anything except who should open the batting for Yorkshire. And when Ben once told me that his grandmother kept a packed suitcase by the front door, I had no idea what he was talking about.

When the bus came to a halt outside the entrance of the concentration camp, we all got off in an uneasy silence and stared up at the uninviting rusty gates. I didn't want to go in, but as everyone else trooped after Mr Costello, I meekly followed. Our first stop was at a vast black wall, where a thousand names had been chiselled into the marble to remind us who had been there only a few years before, and not during a holiday excursion with a tour guide. I saw Ben weeping quietly as he stared at the thirty-seven Levys, three of whom hadn't lived as long as he had. I looked across to see Mark Bairstow looking thoughtful, but apparently unmoved, while the rest of the group remained unusually silent.

The young German guide then took us through the huts that had remained untouched since their occupants were liberated by the Americans. Row upon row of four-tiered bunks, with inch-thick mattresses and no pillows. At one end of the hut, a half-filled bucket of water that had been the lavatory for the fifty-six occupants, emptied once a day. But worse was to come, because Mr Costello had no intention of sparing us.

We climbed back on the bus and took the journey to Hartheim, where our young guide led us into a large soulless building, where we entered a cold eerie room where time had stood still. He pointed to the holes in the ceiling where, he explained, the gas was released into the chamber, but only after the prisoners had been stripped and the doors locked. I felt sick, and didn't have the courage to enter the final room to view the vast ovens that our guard told us had been built in 1933 soon after Hitler had come into power, and where the bodies of his innocent victims were finally turned into dust.

When Ben eventually emerged, he fell to his knees and was violently sick. I thought of his grandmother, and for the first time understood the 'packed suitcase'. I rushed across to join my friend, surprised to find Mark Bairstow already kneeling beside him with an arm around his shoulders, trying to comfort a boy he'd never spoken to before.

★ ★ ★

I was delighted to follow Mark Bairstow as school captain, even if I couldn't hope to

118

emulate his style and panache. I worked diligently during my final year and, with the conscientious help of Mr Costello, was offered a place at Manchester University to read history. I accepted the offer, even though for a Yorkshire-man to cross the Pennines into Lancashire in order to further his education was tantamount to high treason.

By the time I graduated, I didn't need Mr Costello to tell me the profession I was best suited for. And if this tale had been about a schoolmaster, and the years of fulfilment he gained from being a teacher . . . but it isn't.

★ ★ ★

I was teaching at a grammar school in Norfolk when my wife became pregnant, and I had to explain to her why she would have to travel up to Yorkshire to give birth to our son otherwise the lad couldn't play for the county. Not that she had any interest in the game of cricket. It turned out to be a girl, so the subject was never mentioned again. However, I took advantage of being back in Leeds to look up my old friend Ben Levy, now a local solicitor, to suggest we spend a day at Headingley and watch the Roses Match.

Being Yorkshiremen, we were in our seats long before the first ball was bowled, and by the morning break the county were at 77 for two. 'A spot of lunch?' I suggested as I rose from my place in the Hutton stand and glanced up at the President's box to see a face I could have sworn

I recognized, despite the passing of time. But he was wearing a dog collar and purple shirt, which threw me for a moment.

I touched Ben on the elbow and, pointing to the box, said, 'Is that who I think it is?'

'Yes, it's Mark Bairstow, the new Bishop of Ripon. Still loves his cricket.'

'But I always assumed he was destined to be the next chairman of Bairstow's, the finest iron forgers in the county.'

'And therefore the world,' laughed Ben. 'But when he went up to Cambridge, he changed courses in his first term and read theology. So no one was surprised he ended up as a bishop.'

★   ★   ★

Like Mr Costello, I too organized an annual trip to Europe, and after excursions to Rome, Paris and Madrid, I felt the time had come to return to Berlin and see how much the German capital had changed, since the Wall had finally come down.

I found the city was transformed. Only one small graffiti-covered section of the Wall still stood firmly in place, an ugly monument to remind the next generation what their parents and grandparents had endured, which they were now studying as history.

Dresden turned out to be a modern city of steel and glass, and you would have had to search Munich to believe the Germans had ever been involved in a war. And when we visited the Cuvilliés-Theater, two of the boys showed the same excitement that I had felt when I saw my first opera.

When the final day came, I considered, like Mr Costello, it was my duty to visit Dachau, as anti-Semitism was once again rearing its ugly head in my country. I was just as apprehensive as I had been the first time, although I tried not to let the boys and girls know how I felt. When the bus came to a halt outside the main entrance, I silently led the children through the even rustier gates and into the camp, and as far as I could see nothing had changed. My young wards spent some time staring at the names on the memorial wall, and when I saw the thirty-seven Levys, I thought of Ben. The huts remained untouched, and I could see the look of disbelief in the children's eyes when they saw the water bucket at the end of the room. They would never complain again about their cramped dormitories.

Our guide then took us into the museum, where we studied the photographs of prisoners whose black-and-white striped pyjamas hung on their skeletal frames, and of the bodies of lifeless men and women being dragged from the gas chambers to the ovens. There was even a photograph of Himmler to remind us who had carried out Hitler's orders.

I felt sorry for our German guide, not much older than myself, whose sad eyes suggested that the Nazi era couldn't be that easily cast aside, although like myself, he would have been born after the war.

And then the final stage of the tour, which I had been dreading. I still felt sick when I entered the gas chamber, but at least this time I had the courage to follow my wards into the building where the ovens were situated. I stared at the temperature gauges and switches on the wall and bowed my head. When I raised it again, my eyes settled on the large oven door, and I understood for the first time the journey one young man had taken before he became the Bishop of Ripon.

BAIRSTOW & SON

IRON FORGERS

FOUNDED 1866

THE CUCKOLD

Adam Weston and Gareth Blakemore always met on a Sunday evening to share a bottle of wine and put the world to rights.

The venue never changed, only the wine, which was always vintage and selected by Adam. But then he was the proprietor of the Swan Inn, a popular gastropub on the outskirts of Evesham.

Gareth was Adam's oldest friend, a successful lawyer by profession, with chambers in Lincoln's Inn. He'd recently been appointed a QC, and he and his wife Angela lived in a Victorian pile at the the other end of the village. Gareth would usually drop into the Swan around seven, before travelling on to London. Tonight, he was late, very late, and Adam knew why.

Gareth walked in just after nine, looking tired and depressed. He gave his friend a weak smile, before seating himself on a stool at the far end of the bar. Adam uncorked a bottle of wine, poured two glasses and joined his friend.

'What is it?' asked Gareth after taking a sip.

'An underrated Cabernet Sauvignon from Napa Valley that's proving rather popular with my regulars.'

'I can see why,' said Gareth, taking another sip.

'How's your week been?' asked Adam, aware there was no time to waste.

'You don't want to know. Tell me your news, because it's got to be better than mine.'

'We had a good week,' said Adam. 'Greene King have offered me the opportunity to buy the pub, but at the moment I just don't have that sort of money.'

'How much are they asking?'

'Two million. It's a fair price, and the only stipulation they're insisting on is that I continue to sell their beer for the next ten years.'

'That seems fair enough,' said Gareth, 'assuming you made a decent return last year.'

'Turnover was almost a million, and after rent, rates and taxes, I showed a profit of around ninety thousand, not including my salary.'

'Sounds like a worthwhile investment to me.'

'And I have plans to add another dozen or so covers in the restaurant. I've also got my eye on a chef who's working at the Savoy. Tells me he's sick of commuting up and down to London every day.'

'That all seems rather promising, but what's the bank's attitude?'

'They'd loan me a million at four per cent, but would expect to have a lock on all my assets, including the pub. So I still need to raise another million from other sources, and wondered if you'd consider coming in as my partner?'

'I'd love to,' said Gareth, 'but you couldn't have chosen a worse time.'

'But I keep reading in the press that you're one of the most successful barristers in the royal courts.'

'Yes, but not for much longer.'

'How come?'

'Angela's filed for divorce. I have a preliminary meeting with her lawyers tomorrow morning. They're the meanest in the business, and I should know — I recommended them.'

'How come?'

'Angela told me she was asking on behalf of a friend, and the friend turned out to be her.'

'I'm really sorry,' said Adam. 'I had no idea,' he added as he looked across the bar at his old classmate.

'I have to admit that it hasn't been a bundle of laughs lately,' Gareth said, after taking another sip of his drink, 'and I'm mostly to blame. If you spend the week in London and can't always get back at the weekends, it doesn't help.'

'But divorce or no divorce, you must still have a worthwhile income from the bar.'

'And I'm going to need every penny of it,' said Gareth. 'Angela's lawyers are driving a hard bargain. They're demanding the manor house as well as the villa in the south of France, and that's just for starters.'

'But you've still got the Chelsea flat, which must be worth a bob or two,' said Adam.

'True, but I'll need to hold on to it if I'm going to survive,' said Gareth. 'Fortunately she thinks it's rented and I told her it's coming up for renewal next year.'

'Then perhaps it might be wise to settle with her before she finds out how much it's really worth.'

'I'd agree with you in normal circumstances,' said Gareth, lowering his voice, 'if I hadn't just found out she's having an affair. And if I could only discover who the bastard is, I'd be in a stronger position.'

'What makes you so sure she's having an affair?'

'I found a cufflink under the bed, and it certainly wasn't mine.'

★ ★ ★

'Gareth found a cufflink under the bed and told me it wasn't his.'

Angela calmly lit a cigarette. She inhaled deeply before saying, 'Then we'll have to be more careful in the future. If Gareth were to find out we're having an affair, there would be no chance of me getting my hands on the two million my lawyers are demanding. Which would also mean I wouldn't be able to invest in the pub.'

'But you still want to be my partner?' said Adam nervously.

'In every sense of the word, my darling,' Angela replied, blowing out a cloud of smoke. 'But if I don't get hold of that money, I could end up serving behind the bar.'

'That wasn't part of my overall plan,' said Adam. 'Although the moment I can move in with you, I'm going to convert the top floor of the pub into bedrooms, which would bring in some much needed extra income. But I'll need your help when it comes to the interior design.'

'Only too happy to play my part,' said Angela as she stubbed out her cigarette. 'But I still think it would be wise for us to cool it for the time being.' Adam couldn't hide his disappointment.

She leant across and kissed him gently on the lips. 'But once he's signed the divorce papers,' she added, breaking away, 'I'll not only be free to become your partner, but your wife.'

'I can think of another way that would convince him to settle quickly.' Angela raised an eyebrow. 'Demand to see the details of the lease on his flat in Chelsea.'

'No. It's much better he still believes that's his trump card, and in any case, it would only hold up your deal with Greene King.' She lay back on her pillow and pulled the sheet over her. 'How's that going, by the way?'

'I had a meeting with a brewery representative last week, and we agreed terms. They told me as soon as I'm ready to put down a deposit, they'll draw up a contract.'

'Then all you'll need to do on Sunday is convince Gareth that he should come up with the two million, and the pub will be yours.'

'Ours,' said Adam, as he placed a hand on the inside of her leg and slipped back down under the sheet.

★ ★ ★

'It's a burgundy,' said Gareth.

'You'd have known that,' said Adam, 'by just looking at the shape of the bottle.'

Gareth frowned and took another sip. 'I must admit it's quite superb. My bet is a Clos de Tart?'

Adam half nodded. 'Close, try again.'

Gareth took another sip, and looked up at the ceiling as if seeking inspiration. 'Got it. Chambolle-Musigny.'

'Bravo, quite right.'

'In which case, it's about the only thing I've got right this week,' said Gareth, draining his glass.

'That bad?'

'Worse. Angela's upped the ante, and is now demanding two million.'

'Then perhaps it might be wise to settle before she demands more.'

'You may well be right, but if I could only find out who lover boy is, Angela might suddenly become more reasonable.'

'But if she found out about the flat, you could end up having to pay even more, and surely that's not a risk worth taking.'

'Possibly, but I think I'll still give it another week before I finally decide.'

Adam was about to pour him a second glass when Gareth raised a hand. 'Not for me, old chum. I have to be off. I've got a breaking and entering at ten tomorrow morning, and I still haven't read the brief. See you next Sunday.'

'And let's hope it's settled by then,' said Adam, 'one way or the other.'

'It would be if I could only find out who the other cufflink belongs to,' said Gareth, as he jumped off his stool and quickly left the pub.

Adam refilled his own glass, but left it untouched until he saw Gareth's car drive onto the London road. He then took the rest of the bottle through to his office. He picked up the phone and dialled a number he called every Sunday evening.

'He's seriously thinking about coming up with the two million,' said Adam once he'd heard the familiar voice. 'And I warned him of the consequences if you were to find out the real value of the apartment.'

'That sounds encouraging,' said Angela.

'Except that he's going to give it another week in the hope he'll find out who your lover is.'

'So we certainly can't risk seeing each other this week,' said Angela.

'But it's been almost a month,' said Adam plaintively, 'and I can't wait to see you again.'

'I know how you feel, my darling, but it won't be much longer before we can spend the rest of our lives together.'

'Let's hope so.'

'Stop being so pessimistic, Adam. I'll call you the moment I have any news.'

★   ★   ★

'Can you talk?'

'Yes,' whispered Adam.

'He's agreed to the two million.' Adam wanted to scream out loud, but not while the pub was so crowded. 'My lawyers are drawing up a contract,' continued Angela, 'that he's promised to sign on Monday morning, and as you'll be seeing him on Sunday evening, all you have to do is make sure he doesn't change his mind.'

'Not a chance of that,' said Adam. 'I've even

131

selected his favourite bottle of wine for the occasion.'

'Why don't you put a bottle of champagne on ice at the same time, and if he does sign on Monday, you could join me for dinner and we can celebrate by spending our first night together in your new home?'

★ ★ ★

Adam had been standing impatiently by the phone for some time before it eventually rang. He grabbed the receiver.

'He's just left the house so should be with you in a few minutes.'

'Why's he so late?' asked Adam edgily. 'I was beginning to think he might have found out about us and driven straight up to London.'

'You're over-reacting again, my darling,' said Angela. 'He just had rather a lot of packing to do before he finally left.'

'That's a relief, because I can't stall the brewery for much longer.'

'I'm sure they can wait until Monday.'

'And if you can call me the moment he's signed, I'll put down the deposit of two hundred thousand they're demanding, though I confess it will clear me out.'

'No need to worry yourself about that, my darling. Once he's signed I'll immediately transfer a million to your account and the pub will be yours.'

'Ours,' Adam reminded her, as he watched Gareth's Jaguar driving into the car park. 'He's just arrived,' he whispered.

'Good. Just make sure he doesn't change his mind.'

'No fear of that,' said Adam before putting down the phone. He bent down and extracted a dusty bottle of 1987 Pouilly-Fumé from under the counter. He'd uncorked it by the time Gareth marched in, looking happy for the first time in months.

'No need for you to guess this week,' said Adam, placing two glasses on the bar in front of him. 'Because I've chosen one of your favourites.'

'What are we celebrating?'

'Your freedom, of course.'

'How could you possibly know about that?' said Gareth.

'I could tell from the expression on your face,' said Adam, a little too quickly. 'So it will be just like old times,' he added, raising his glass.

'Not quite. I still have to sign the document tomorrow morning.'

'But surely you're not having second thoughts?'

'I was, but decided on balance to take your advice and try to move on.'

'Even though it's going to cost you two million?'

'Along with the family home and our villa in the south of France.'

'Well, at least you still have the Chelsea flat.'

'And a cufflink,' said Gareth.

'A cufflink?'

'Don't you remember, the proof that Angela's having an affair?'

'Ah, yes,' said Adam. 'I remember.'

'And what's more, I'm fairly certain I now know who owns the other one.'

Adam could feel his cheeks going red. He quickly took a gulp of wine. 'Anyone we know?'

'No.'

'Then, how do — '

'Because I found two BA tickets for a flight to Nice in her handbag.'

Adam didn't speak as Gareth put a hand in his trouser pocket, took out a cufflink and placed it on the bar. Adam stared at a blue and silver crested cufflink.

'I suspect that lover boy will be joining her at Heathrow tomorrow morning, before they go on to our — her — villa in the south of France.'

Adam continued to stare at a cufflink he'd never seen before.

THE HOLIDAY OF
A LIFETIME

'Stop nagging, woman,' said Dennis, but not loudly enough for his wife to hear.

Dennis Pascoe would have got divorced years ago, but couldn't afford to. He'd been married to Joyce for thirty-four years, and assumed it must now, unfortunately, be till death do us part.

She hadn't been his first choice, but then he suspected he hadn't been hers. Dennis used to tell himself they'd stayed together because of the children, but that was no longer convincing, as both Joanna and Ken now lived abroad, so the truth was they remained together because of inertia.

Dennis had recently retired as the deputy station master at Audley End, a branch line for Saffron Walden. It hadn't exactly been an earth-shattering career. He'd left school at fourteen, with no qualifications, and failed several interviews for other jobs before he signed on as an apprentice with British Rail. He told his mother Audley End was no more than a stepping stone for something bigger. The problem was, Dennis had no idea what that something bigger might be, and never found out.

Dennis progressed from apprentice, to ticket collector, to booking clerk, finally ending up as deputy station master in charge of a team of five. Only three of them on duty at any one time. In reality, 'deputy' meant he couldn't afford to join

137

the local golf club, and was unlikely to be invited to become a Rotarian.

However, the real problem came when Great Eastern took over the franchise from BR and Dennis opted for early retirement on a full pension at the age of fifty-five, convinced he was still young enough to find another job to supplement his meagre income. Wrong again, because there weren't many jobs in the private sector for retired deputy station masters, other than as a night watchman or a lollipop man, both of which Joyce wouldn't allow him to consider.

Within days of retirement, Dennis also discovered that marriage may well have been ordained for better or worse, but not for seven days a week. Joyce, who had never done a day's work in her life — other than to keep the house clean, do the shopping, feed him, handle all the household bills and bring up the children — didn't appreciate Dennis getting under her feet while she was trying to do the housework. Housewives don't retire, she often reminded him.

The other problem Dennis had to face was that his pension didn't allow him to indulge in many luxuries and, with inflation, that was only likely to get worse as he approached old age. He had a season ticket for Norwich Football Club at the wrong end of the ground, which he could just about afford, and their fortunes were not much better than his. They were either trying to survive in the first division or attempting to reach the play-offs in the second. And then there was the love of his life, not Joyce, but his stamp collection — a hobby that had begun at the age of seven, when his grandfather had given him a packet of 'Commonwealth Specials' to celebrate the Queen's coronation. Dennis now had over a thousand examples of stamps from all over the world, proudly mounted in five separate albums.

His only other extravagance was to subscribe to Stanley Gibbons' monthly newsletter and catalogue, which he then spent hours perusing, aware that he would never be able to afford the rare examples he would have most liked to add to his collection.

Dennis tried to fill his day with long walks, not always possible when it was raining, and a visit to the local pub, where he sat in the corner drinking a half pint of bitter slowly, while reading the *Sun*. He made sure he was back in time for lunch, after which he migrated to the sofa only to fall asleep while watching afternoon television or turning the pages of his stamp albums.

It was while Dennis was reading the *Sun* and Joyce was vacuuming the front room that he spotted the advertisement for a package holiday on the Costa del Sol, which sounded a lot more exciting than their annual visit to Skegness. Dennis studied the advertisement more carefully, while Joyce attempted to vacuum around him. They were offering bed and full board, flights included, for £200. Too good to be true, thought Dennis, but would Joyce even consider the prospect? During his morning walk, he thought about how to convince her the time had come to be a little more adventurous.

Dennis waited until the end of lunch before he said, 'Damn good sausage and mash, luv.' Joyce looked suspicious, as praise didn't often flow from that side of the table, so she could only wonder what he was after. She didn't have to wait long to find out. 'I was thinking you might like a change from Skeggie this year,' he suggested.

'What did you have in mind, Dennis, a fortnight in Venice perhaps? A leisurely drive along the Corniche? Possibly a trip down the Nile before stopping off in Cairo to see the treasures of Tutankhamun?'

Dennis ignored the sarcasm and pushed his newspaper across the table to show her the photograph of a villa on the Costa del Sol. Before Joyce could offer an opinion, Dennis added, 'And don't forget, even the train journey to Heathrow will be free.' A deputy station master's perk, he reminded her.

Joyce actually thought it was one of his brighter ideas, just a pity she would have to spend the fortnight with Dennis, but nevertheless she agreed he could look into it.

★ ★ ★

Mr and Mrs Pascoe set out from Audley End for their summer vacation with mixed emotions, so were pleasantly surprised when it turned out to be, as stated boldly in the advertisement, the holiday of a lifetime. They both enjoyed joining the jet set, even if it was only Ryanair, and landing in a country where the sun only left the

140

sky at night; something you couldn't always guarantee in Skegness, even in the summer.

Their room couldn't have been described as luxurious, but it was clean and comfortable, and the three meals a day never once included sausage and mash. Joyce may have been past her bikini days and her husband had bulges in all the wrong places, but at least the beach was not littered with empty beer bottles, while stepping into the sea was like taking a warm bath, and, an added bonus, they made lots of new friends. Whenever Joyce was asked what her husband did, she told them he was a retired station master.

Two weeks later, Mr and Mrs Pascoe returned to England tanned, relaxed and already looking forward to repeating the experience in a year's time; possibly, Joyce suggested, they might even consider going further afield.

The perfect holiday might have been ruined at the last moment when they had to hang around in the baggage hall at Stansted waiting for Dennis's suitcase to appear on the carousel. It didn't. But all was not lost, because when Joyce read the small print on the holiday brochure later that evening, it claimed all losses under £50 were covered by insurance, and as the suitcase had belonged to her mother, and contained little of any real value, she could not have been more delighted when a cheque for thirty-four pounds and fifty-five pence dropped on the mat three weeks later.

Joyce, being a frugal housewife, waited for the January sales before she bought a new suitcase and a handbag she wouldn't have considered in normal circumstances, and even felt a little guilty about. That was until she discovered Dennis had purchased a set of Prince of Wales commemoration stamps without telling her.

★ ★ ★

All would have been well in the Pascoe household, if the missing suitcase had not been found in lost luggage and later returned to Railway Cuttings. Dennis immediately wrote to inform the insurance company, who replied with a standard letter addressed to 'Dear Sir or Madam', above which were stamped the words 'CASE CLOSED'.

Joyce was relieved that they wouldn't have to return the £34 that she'd already spent, but it did make her wonder . . .

Dennis spent the following month writing to all the leading travel companies, and the next six studying the different brochures they all sent by return of post. He took the task seriously, as if he was preparing for an examination, Joyce being the examiner. But it was still some time before he was ready to suggest to his wife where they should spend their next summer holiday.

Joyce also sent away for several brochures, and studied them just as intently, so that by the time Dennis was ready to present his findings on when and where they should go that year, she was equally prepared to tell him what she'd been up to for the past six months.

After a long discussion they settled on

Lanzarote, and that was when Joyce shared with her husband a refinement that she felt would make the holiday even more rewarding. Dennis listened in disbelief to what his wife had in mind, and immediately dismissed the idea out of hand. After all, he said, it's dishonest. However, a week later, after several long walks and too many lingering half pints in the local pub, he asked Joyce to talk him through the idea once again. But it wasn't until he'd studied the latest Stanley Gibbons catalogue and spotted a Penny Black he coveted, that he agreed to go along with her suggestion.

Joyce had clearly given the matter a great deal of thought, and took Dennis carefully through what they would have to do, minute by minute, while allowing her husband to ask questions and point out any weaknesses in her plan. Dennis could only come up with one problem he considered was insurmountable, but was surprised to find that his wife had even thought of a way around that. Dennis was impressed, and even though he still had his doubts, he allowed her to go ahead and fill in all the necessary forms.

★ ★ ★

When Mr and Mrs Pascoe stepped onto the train for Heathrow they were both looking forward to the second 'holiday of a lifetime', and indeed, the break might have gone even better if Dennis had stopped fretting about the consequences of something going wrong with Joyce's plan. But by

143

the time they returned home a fortnight later, they both agreed Lanzarote had turned out to be even more enjoyable than the Costa del Sol. And whenever the subject had arisen, Dennis didn't deny he'd recently retired as a director of Great Eastern, which sounded quite convincing in Lanzarote.

After everyone on their flight had collected their luggage from the carousel, Joyce burst into tears and Dennis did everything he could to console her. She then explained to a sympathetic young baggage handler that one of her suitcases had not appeared on the carousel. An extensive search was carried out, but no one seemed able to find the missing bag. Joyce continued to sob.

Once they were back in Saffron Walden, Joyce waited for a couple of days before she posted two claims for a lost suitcase to two different insurance companies, listing the contents as three dresses, several items of underwear, two pairs of shoes, a bottle of perfume, a washbag and even a lucky charm bracelet (photo attached).

Two cheques, one for £84.20 and a second for £110, arrived within days of each other. The cheques were deposited in two different banks in two different names.

During the Christmas sales, Joyce purchased half a dozen new suitcases of varying sizes from several different department stores in central London, while Dennis acquired an unperforated set of Penny Reds, which he proudly added to his collection.

★ ★ ★

Cunard couldn't have been more apologetic about mislaying one of Mr and Mrs Pascoe's large suitcases — green and clearly labelled Joyce Pascoe, she insisted — while it was being taken off the ship after their third voyage. The purser assured Mrs Pascoe that everything would be done to find it.

A few weeks later, the first of several cheques arrived to cover the loss, while further payments for the same suitcase began to appear at regular intervals over the next six months, as did rarer and rarer, mint and franked, stamps from Stanley Gibbons.

'We mustn't get too greedy,' said Joyce after returning from a winter break in the Caribbean, a holiday that yielded nine further cheques.

So successful were their 'holidays of a lifetime' that after five years, they had accumulated more than enough to make it possible for them to move out of their rented semi-detached in Saffron Walden and buy a small thatched cottage, which they named The Sidings, in Steeple Bumpstead, where Joyce felt they were more likely to come across the sort of people they met on vacation.

* * *

When the Pascoes sat down to plan their next summer holiday, Joyce warned her husband she was beginning to run out of insurance companies, as she couldn't afford to make a claim to the same one twice. Dennis was disappointed by this news, because he'd recently joined the local golf club, acquired a season ticket for Norwich City FC, quite near the centre line, and been invited to become a vice president of Rotary. He'd also begun to stick rarer and rarer stamps into his eighth album. Dennis would have been the first to accept that none of this would have been possible had it not been for his new-found wealth. He realized that he'd climbed onto a bandwagon that he didn't want to get off.

★　★　★

Joyce woke her husband in the middle of the night when she came up with her latest idea. Dennis listened intently and couldn't get back to sleep. If they pulled it off, he might even consider standing for the parish council.

'It will have to be our last job,' she warned her husband, 'because there are only three major insurers left.' She didn't add, whom we haven't robbed.

Joyce wrote out a list of jobs Dennis had to do before they embarked on their summer holiday, including taking out any spare cash they had in their bank accounts. She checked the small print of the three insurance companies where they hadn't made a claim, while Dennis told his friends at the golf club and Rotary that he and Joyce were planning a trip down the Nile to celebrate their fortieth wedding anniversary, because his wife had always wanted to see the Pyramids and visit Tutankhamun's tomb.

Once Joyce had filled in all the forms, and the

letters and cheques had been dispatched, everything was in place by the time they set off for Southampton.

On 17 July 2001, Dennis and Joyce boarded the SS *Balmoral*, which was setting out on a voyage to Salalah, Port Said, and through the Suez Canal, before returning to Southampton via Istanbul.

AUTHOR'S NOTE

At this point in the story I came up with three different endings, and because I couldn't choose between them, decided to write all three and leave you to pick which one you prefer.

A

When the ship docked in Istanbul, several passengers leant over the railings and watched with interest as two police officers climbed aboard the luxury liner, and asked the purser for the number of Mr and Mrs Pascoe's cabin.

Joyce burst into tears when she and Dennis were escorted off the ship and driven to the nearest airport. She didn't stop weeping on the flight to Heathrow, or when a black limousine drove them back to Steeple Bumpstead.

When the Barrington courtesy car pulled up outside the front gate of The Sidings, Joyce burst into tears once again. Dennis climbed out of the car and said nothing as he stared at the smouldering remains of what was left of their little home.

The local fire chief, a fellow Rotarian, hurried across to join them.

'I'm so sorry, Dennis,' he said. 'My men got here as quickly as they could, but once the flames touched the thatched roof, there was little they could do about it.'

'I'm sure you did everything you possibly could, Alan,' said Dennis, trying to look suitably distressed.

'But we've lost everything,' Joyce told a reporter from the local paper, 'and no amount of money will compensate for that.' A quote that was reported on the front page next to a photo of a tearful Joyce, who felt confident the insurance companies wouldn't have missed it. Well, not everything, thought Dennis, because he'd hidden the stamp collection in his locker at the golf club.

Joyce and Dennis booked into the Bumpstead Arms (covered by one of the three insurance policies) and then spent the next month looking for a new home. The company that had insured their contents settled fairly quickly, while the buildings claim took a little longer.

Once Mr and Mrs Pascoe had purchased a similar cottage on the other side of the village, not thatched — too risky, Dennis told his friends at the golf club — and furnished it, there was more than enough left over to live a very comfortable existence, as well as enjoy the occasional off-peak-season holiday while no longer having to mislay any of their luggage.

However, a problem arose that neither of them had anticipated. Boredom set in, and they quickly began to get on each other's nerves again.

It was Joyce who came up with a solution to which Dennis happily agreed. They would change their name, move to the West Country, and once again start looking for 'the holiday of a lifetime'.

B

The first port of call on their trip to the Middle East was Salalah, where they hired a taxi to take them to the souk. They took their time strolling around the crowded bazaar, with its hundreds of colourful market stalls, displaying thousands of different-quality carpets. But Joyce was far more interested in finding the right dealer than the right carpet. Once they'd selected a man who wouldn't have been invited to give a talk at the Rotary club, they joined him for a cup of Turkish coffee before the bargaining could begin for an exquisite, thousand-thread silk carpet that the dealer claimed was unique.

An hour later Joyce agreed on a sum, which Dennis paid in cash. The dealer then supplied them with a receipt for four times the amount they had paid for the rare silk carpet.

In Port Said, they visited several emporiums, and selected only the finest pieces of jewellery, including a gold brooch of Nefertiti, a string of pearls worthy of Cleopatra, and a diamond-studded bracelet that Joyce felt confident would be the envy of her fellow lady Rotarians. The proprietors were equally obliging when it came to the receipts. Replacement value for insurance purposes, Joyce explained.

In Istanbul, they purchased an oil painting of a fishing boat on the Bosphorus that Joyce felt would look perfect above the mantelpiece in their front room, and although the price was exorbitant, triple the amount was entered on the receipt.

By the time the *Balmoral* docked in Southampton, the Pascoes had spent all their spare cash, but they now possessed some extremely valuable merchandise, and Joyce had the receipts to prove it.

Joyce took her time packing everything they'd bought on the trip into a large green suitcase before a porter arrived to pick up their trunk and two other smaller suitcases. When the Pascoes arrived in the baggage hall, Joyce gave a farewell performance worthy of Elizabeth Taylor.

'One large green suitcase, you say, madam?'

'Yes,' said Joyce, 'full of all the beautiful things we bought on the trip.' Dennis appeared to be making every effort to comfort his wife, something he was getting rather good at.

After the promise of a reward, several members of the ship's crew set out in search of a large green suitcase, but an hour later, no one was able to claim the reward.

The Pascoes were among the last to leave the baggage hall, but not before they were convinced there was no longer any hope of finding their missing treasures. A porter placed their trunk and the two other suitcases on a trolley and began pushing it towards the exit.

Dennis and Joyce trudged mournfully after him, and as if to add insult to injury, a recently promoted Customs officer pulled them to one side and asked them to place their luggage on the counter. The porter obeyed without hesitation.

'May I ask if you purchased anything of value while you were abroad, madam?'

'No,' Joyce said, 'just a few souvenirs. Nothing of any real value.'

She happily opened the two suitcases to reveal Dennis's dirty laundry and washbag in one, and her neatly folded clothes in the other.

'Thank you,' he said. 'And the trunk?' The porter once again heaved it up onto the counter.

'Would you open it, please, sir,' said the Customs officer, as Dennis turned to look at his wife.

Once again Joyce burst into tears, but this time she wasn't greeted with the same sympathetic look.

'Would you please open the trunk, sir,' the young officer repeated a little more firmly.

After what seemed an eternity, Dennis reluctantly stepped forward, unlocked the trunk and pushed up the lid to reveal a large green suitcase that almost took up the entire space.

'Would you now open the suitcase,' said the young man, as a more senior officer walked across to join them.

Dennis unzipped the suitcase and slowly lifted the lid to reveal all the carefully selected purchases they had made during the past fortnight. The junior officer started to take them out and unwrap them one by one, while the senior officer began to make a note of each item. He spoke for the first time.

'Have you kept any receipts for these souvenirs?' he asked.

'Yes,' said Dennis.

'No,' said Joyce, which caused the senior officer to ask the woman to hand over her bag, where he quickly found an envelope stuffed with forty-two receipts.

He took his time checking each item before transferring the amounts onto a large calculator. It was some time before he declared, 'You may wish to check my figures, madam, but I think you'll find the overall amount comes to twenty-seven thousand, seven hundred and sixteen pounds. Now, I am sure you are both aware there is a forty per cent import tax levied on any goods purchased while abroad, above the cost of fifty pounds.' He returned to his calculator. 'Which means you are liable to pay Her Majesty's Customs and Excise eleven thousand and eighty-six pounds and forty pence. Should you be unable to do so, all the goods will be confiscated until you have covered the full amount.'

C

During the train journey back to Audley End, Dennis and Joyce agreed it was the best holiday they'd ever been on, and were already planning where they should go next year.

Joyce felt it might be wise to take a taxi back to Steeple Bumpstead rather than drag all the suitcases on and off the bus. Dennis agreed, although he was down to his last ten pounds.

When the taxi pulled up outside the front gate of The Sidings, Joyce collapsed in tears.

Dennis climbed out of the taxi, and said nothing as he stared at the smouldering remains of what was left of their little cottage.

The local fire chief, a fellow Rotarian, hurried across to join them.

'I'm so sorry, Dennis,' he said. 'My men got here as quickly as they could, but once the flames touched the thatched roof, there was little they could do about it.'

'I'm sure you did everything you possibly could, Alan,' said Dennis, trying to look suitably distressed.

Joyce didn't stop crying, and Dennis wondered if she wasn't overdoing it. 'Look on the bright side,' he whispered, placing an arm around his wife's shoulder, 'No doubt you took out several policies on the house.'

'But I didn't insure the house,' said Joyce with feeling. 'Never could see much point.'

DOUBLE OR QUITS

'I think we've got a problem on table number three,' said the manager, staring intently at the screen on his desk.

'Which punter?' asked the head of security, as he joined his boss and looked over his shoulder.

'Young guy, with an attractive woman standing behind him. What do you think, André?'

'Zoom in,' said the security chief, 'and let's take a closer look.' The manager touched a button and waited until the young man's face filled the screen. 'I agree,' said André, 'he's a double or quits merchant. I think from the sweat on his forehead, he's probably got a lot riding on it.'

'And the girl?' said the manager, as he switched the camera to a young woman, whose right hand rested on the gambler's shoulder.

'All I can tell you is she's not a one-night stand.'

'How can you be sure?'

'They're both wearing wedding rings.'

'Get Duval up here.'

André quickly left the room as the manager of the casino watched the young man place another thousand francs on 13.

'Idiot,' said the manager, as he glanced at the front page of *Le Figaro*, which was on the desk by his side. He didn't need to read the article a third time. The headline was bad enough.

ELEVENTH SUICIDE REPORTED IN MONTE CARLO FOLLOWING HEAVY GAMBLING LOSSES

He looked back at the screen to see the young punter place a further thousand francs on 13. 'Idiot,' he repeated. 'Haven't I got enough problems without you?'

Claude Richelieu, the owner of the casino, had been on the phone from Paris earlier in the week, concerned about the latest government directive. The French interior minister was pressing the Monte Carlo gaming council to close the recently opened casino. Too many stories in the press about suicides, broken marriages and bankruptcies caused by gambling, which was illegal in France, and precisely the reason why they were making so much money in Monte Carlo. The manager had cursed when Richelieu added, 'We don't need any more suicides.'

'But what am I supposed to do,' he asked, 'if someone loses badly and then decides to kill themselves?'

'Fix the wheel,' said Richelieu. 'Make sure he wins.'

'And if that fails?'

The owner told his manager exactly what he should do if fixing the wheel wasn't enough.

There was a knock on the door, and the head of security returned, accompanied by one of the few members of staff who wasn't wearing a dinner jacket that evening. In fact, if you had passed Philippe Duval in the street, you might have thought the short, balding middle-aged man was a schoolmaster, or perhaps an accountant. But he had other talents that were far more valuable to the casino. Mr Duval could lip-read in five different languages.

'Which one?' he asked, as he stared down at the screen.

'The young guy,' said the manager, once again zooming in on him. 'What can you tell me about him?'

Duval watched carefully, but it was some time before he offered an opinion, during which the young man had lost another thousand francs on 13. 'He's French,' Duval eventually said, 'a Parisian, and the lady standing behind him is his wife, Maxine, unless they're both married to someone else.'

'Tell me what they're saying,' said Marcel.

Duval leant forward and watched carefully.

'Him, 'My luck's got to change soon.'

'Her, 'I'd rather you stopped, Jacques. Let's go back to the hotel while we've still got enough money to pay the bill.'

'Him, 'It's not the hotel bill I'm worried about, as you well know, Maxine. It's that loan shark who'll be waiting for me the moment I show my face in Paris.''

The young man placed another thousand francs on 13. The ball landed on 26.

'Him, 'Next time.''

'Is Tony on tonight?' the manager asked.

'Yes, boss,' replied the head of security. 'Table nine.'

'Switch him with the guy on table three, and tell him to make sure the ball lands in 13.'

'He's still only got a one in five chance,' said

161

the head of security.

'That's better than thirty-seven to one,' said the manager. 'Get on with it.'

'On my way, boss,' said the head of security. He hurried out of the room and headed down to the casino floor, but not before the young man had lost another thousand francs.

'Pull the camera back,' said Duval. The manager zoomed out. 'I want to take a closer look at that man leaning against the pillar in the far corner.' The camera moved onto a middle-aged man who was also staring intently at the table. 'He's that journalist from *Le Figaro*.'

'Are you sure?' the manager barked.

'Look at the photo next to his byline on the front page,' he said, tapping the newspaper on the desk.

'François Colbert,' said the manager. 'I could kill him.'

'I think that's what he has in mind for you,' said Duval, as the camera returned to the roulette table, where two of the croupiers were swapping stations.

'Make it land in 13, Tony,' said the manager as the new croupier began to spin the wheel. While everyone's eyes were on the ball, the croupier's right hand slipped under the table.

Jacques placed another thousand francs on 13, as the croupier sent the little white ball on its way. The young man, the manager, the head of security and Duval all followed the progress of the ball, which ended up in 27, one slot to the left of 13.

'He'll get it right next time,' said the manager.

'He'd better,' said Duval, 'because the mark's only got two chips left.'

The young man put them both on 13. Once again, the croupier sent the ball spinning, and once again his index finger felt for the hidden lever under the table, as six people with a vested interest watched to see where the ball would land. 36.

'Now Tony's managed both sides of thirteen,' said the manager, 'surely he'll get it right a third time.'

'But I think our guy's run out of money,' said Duval, as the young man swung round to face his wife.

'What's he saying?' demanded the manager.

'I can't tell you while he's got his back to me. But zoom in on the woman. She's saying, 'But it's all I've got left, Jacques, and if I let you have it, we'll be cleaned out.''

The croupier once again spun the wheel and released the ball before flicking the lever of the trip pin a third time, when the ball finally landed in 13, but the gambler hadn't had time to place a bet. As the young man turned back, a gasp went up from those standing around the table, and he said in despair, 'If only you'd believed in me, Maxine, I could have won the three hundred thousand I needed to clear my debt.'

The young woman quickly unclasped her bag and handed over a wad of notes to the croupier. He counted them slowly.

'Ten thousand francs, sir?' he said impassively, before dropping the money into a plastic box by his side.

'Keep your eye on the journalist,' said Duval. The manager glanced across at François Colbert, who was writing down every word Jacques and his wife were saying.

'*Merde!*' he said, and turned his attention back to the croupier.

'Put it all on 13,' said the young man.

The croupier glanced across at the deputy manager, who nodded. He spun the wheel and released the ball, feeling for the lever once more. It landed in 13, but only for a moment before it popped back out and settled in 27. The young man let out a piercing scream, and as he stood up and left the table, yelled at the woman, 'You've left me with no choice.'

Maxine collapsed into the nearest chair and burst into tears, as her husband ran out of the back of the casino and onto the terrace. The manager left his desk and walked quickly out onto the balcony. He watched as the young man ran out onto the beach, and continued running towards the sea. The manager looked more closely, and could have sworn he was holding a gun in his right hand.

He quickly returned to his desk and was trying to get his security chief on the phone, when he heard a single shot ring out.

'Get back up here,' said the manager when André came on the line. 'And quickly.'

The manager walked over to a large safe embedded in the wall. He entered an eight-digit code and pulled open the heavy door. 'How much did he say would solve his problems?'

'Three hundred thousand francs,' said Duval,

as André burst into the room.

'Take this money,' said the manager, handing over an armful of cash, 'and carry out the boss's orders.'

The security chief slipped out of the room, walked down the back stairs and out of a rear entrance onto the beach. He quickly identified a set of fresh prints in the moonlight, and followed them until he came to a body lying in the sand, blood pouring out of his mouth, a pistol by his side. The head of security looked up to check no one was watching him, before he began to stuff wads of cash into the dead man's jacket pockets, and then his trouser pockets, finally leaving a few francs scattered in the sand by his side.

André double-checked to make sure no one had seen what he'd done, before he got off his knees and made his way back towards the casino. Once inside, he ran up the back stairs and into the manager's office.

'Job done,' was all he said.

'Good. Now no one will be able to suggest he committed suicide because he lost heavily at the tables.'

★   ★   ★

Maxine waited until the head of security had disappeared back into the casino, before she made her way out onto the beach. She kept glancing back to be sure no one was watching her.

When she found the body, she knelt down on the sand, and began to extract the francs from his pockets, before placing the bundles of cash in a large empty handbag. She even picked up the few stray ones that were lying by his side.

Maxine knelt down and kissed her husband gently on the forehead. 'The coast is clear, my darling,' she whispered, glancing back up towards the casino.

Jacques opened his eyes and smiled. 'I'll see you and François back in Paris,' he said as his wife picked up the bag and slipped quickly away.

THE SENIOR
VICE PRESIDENT

1

Arthur Dunbar studied Mr S. Macpherson's account with some considerable satisfaction, bordering on pride. His eyes returned to the bottom line: $8,681,762. He checked it against last year's figure, $8,189,614. An increase of 6 per cent, and one mustn't forget that during the past year his client had spent $281,601 on personal expenditure, which included all his household bills, and a quarterly payment to a Mr and Mrs Laidlaw, who, Arthur assumed, must be his long-serving staff.

Arthur leant back in his chair, and not for the first time thought about the man who hailed from Ambrose in the Highlands of Scotland. When Arthur had first been given the responsibility of handling the account, some eighteen years ago, all his predecessor had told him was that a man, not much older than Arthur was at the time, had turned up at the bank and, having made a fortune on the railroad, deposited $871,000 in cash, and announced he was going home to Scotland.

It made Arthur smile to think that anyone who turned up with $10,000 in cash today would be subject to an investigation by their recently formed money-laundering team, and if they didn't tick all the boxes, their file would be handed over to the Toronto police's special investigation squad.

Arthur had long ago stopped trying to fathom why Mr Macpherson still did business with the National Bank of Toronto, when there were so many Scottish banks that were just as competent and considerably more convenient. But as he had conducted his affairs in an exemplary fashion for the past twenty-five years, the subject no longer arose, and in any case, NBT wouldn't have wanted to lose one of their most important customers.

Although Arthur knew very little about his client other than that they both shared the same heritage, one thing he had learnt over the years was that he was unquestionably a shrewd, intelligent businessman. After all, he had multiplied his original investment tenfold, while at the same time withdrawing enough money to live an extremely comfortable lifestyle. In fact, only once in the past eighteen years had he failed to show a profit, despite stock market collapses, changes of governments and countless skirmishes around the globe. He appeared to have no vices, and his only extravagance was purchasing the occasional painting from Munro's, a fine art dealer in Edinburgh — and then only if it was by a Scottish artist.

Arthur had long ago accepted he didn't have Mr Macpherson's flair for finance, but he was quite happy to sit at the feet of the master and when any new instructions came, he would invest a portion of his own money in the same shares at a level no one would have noticed. So when the bank's senior vice president checked his own account at the end of the quarter, it stood at $243,519. How he would have liked to thank Mr Macpherson in person, because retirement was fast approaching for Arthur, and with his little nest egg and a full pension, he looked forward to ending his days in a degree of comfort he felt he had earned.

If there was a Mrs Macpherson there were no clues to suggest it, so Arthur rather assumed that, like him, his client was a bachelor. But like so many mysteries surrounding the man, he didn't know for sure, and assumed he never would.

However, something had been worrying Arthur about the account for some weeks, though he couldn't put a finger on it. He opened the file again and noted the figure, $8,681,762, before checking every entry meticulously. But all seemed to be in order.

He then studied each cheque that the different individuals and companies had presented during the past month, before checking them against the entries in the ledger. Every one tallied. All the usual household expenses and utility bills, food, wine, gas, electricity, even Hudsons, the local newsagent. But he still felt something wasn't quite right. And then, in the middle of the night, it hit him like a thunderbolt. Less, not more.

On arrival at the bank the following morning, the first thing Arthur did was to take Mr Macpherson's ledger out of the bottom drawer. He turned the pages back to the previous quarter, and was able to confirm the most recent bills were considerably less than those for any other quarter. Had they been considerably more, Arthur would have spotted it immediately, and become suspicious. The fact that they were less, aroused his interest. The only entry that remained consistent was the monthly banker's order for his long-serving retainers, Mr and Mrs Laidlaw.

He leant back in his chair and wondered if he should inform the manager of this break in routine, but decided against it for two reasons. It was coming up to quarter day, when he would receive his new instructions from Mr Macpherson, and with it no doubt a simple explanation as to why the bills had fallen, and second, he didn't care much for the new manager of the bank.

There had been a time, not so very long ago, when Arthur had considered the possibility of being appointed manager himself, but his hopes were dashed when that position was filled by a Mr Stratton from their Montreal branch, who was half his age, but a graduate of McGill and the Wharton Business School. Arthur on the other hand had, to quote his late father — a former sergeant in the Seaforth Highlanders — risen through the ranks, and quite recently acquired the title of senior vice president. However, everyone in banking circles knew there were several vice presidents, and you only became the senior VP because everyone else had retired and you were next in line. 'Buggins' turn', as his father would have described it.

Arthur had applied to be the manager of one of the bank's smaller branches a couple of times, but hadn't even made the shortlist. On one occasion he'd overheard a member of the panel say, 'Dunbar's a good enough chap but simply isn't officer material.'

He had also considered leaving NBT to join one of their rivals, but quickly discovered he wouldn't be starting at the same salary, and he certainly couldn't hope to be offered the same pension plan as he was entitled to after so many years of loyal and devoted service. After all, in eighteen months' time he would have been with the bank for thirty years, which meant he could retire on two-thirds of his current salary; less than thirty years, and it would only be half. So he only had to cling on for another eighteen months.

Arthur turned his attention back to the pile of cheques on his desk, and was about to go over them once again, when the phone rang. He picked it up and immediately recognized the cheerful voice of Barbara, Mr Stratton's secretary.

'Mr Stratton wondered if you could pop round and see him when it's convenient — ' code for as soon as possible — 'as there's something he'd like to discuss with you fairly urgently — ' code for now.

'Of course,' said Arthur. 'I'll be with you in a moment.'

He disliked being summoned to the manager's office because it was rarely, if ever, good news. Last time Stratton had called for him was when he needed a volunteer to organize the Christmas party, and the responsibility had ended up taking hours of his spare time without any remuneration, and gone were the days when he could hope that one of the girls from the typing pool would go home with him later that evening.

The happiest of these occasions was when

Barbara had joined the bank, and they had what might be described as a fling. He found they had so much in common, even enjoying the same passion for classical music, although he still couldn't understand why she preferred Brahms to Beethoven. And the biggest regret in Arthur's life was that he didn't ask her to marry him. When she married Reg Caldercroft in accounts, he ended up as best man.

He closed the Macpherson file and placed it in the top drawer of his desk, which he locked. He left his room and walked slowly down the corridor, knocked on the manager's door and received a curt 'Come' in response. Something else he didn't like about Mr Stratton.

Arthur opened the door and entered a large, well-furnished office, and waited to be told he could sit down. Stratton smiled up at him and pointed to the chair on the other side of his desk. Arthur returned the smile, equally insincere, wondering what voluntary chore was about to be thrust upon him.

'Good morning, Arthur,' said the young man.

'Good morning, Mr Stratton,' replied Arthur, who had once addressed him as Gerald when he first took over as manager, only to be told, 'not during working hours'. And as they never met socially, it was also the last time he had addressed the manager by his Christian name.

'Arthur,' he said, the same smile. 'I've had a letter from head office that I felt I ought to share with you, remembering that you are the bank's senior vice president and our longest-serving member of staff.'

What's he after? was Arthur's first thought.

'I have been instructed to make cutbacks on staff. The figure they are insisting on,' Stratton said, looking down at a letter on his desk, 'is ten per cent. And the board are recommending we start by offering senior staff the opportunity to take early retirement.'

To make way for younger people who they will only have to pay half the salary, Arthur wanted to say, but kept his counsel.

'And of course, I thought you might consider this an ideal opportunity, after your little scare last year.'

'It wasn't a scare,' said Arthur, 'and I was off work for four days. The only four days in nearly thirty years with the bank,' he reminded Stratton.

'Indeed, most commendable,' said Stratton. 'But don't you think these things are sometimes a warning?'

'No, I do not,' said Arthur. 'I've never felt fitter, and as you well know, I only need to serve another eighteen months to qualify for a full pension.'

'I realize that,' said Stratton, 'and please don't think I'm not sympathetic. But my hands are tied.' He looked down at the letter, clearly trying to place the blame on someone else. 'I'm sure you'll appreciate the problem I'm facing . . .'

'It's me who's facing the problem, not you,' said Arthur, bolder than he'd ever been in the past.

'And the board asked me to say,' said Stratton, 'how much they appreciate the long and dedicated service you have given the bank. And I feel sure you'll be pleased to know they have agreed that a farewell party should be thrown in your honour, along with an appropriate gift to mark your remarkable service to the National Bank of Toronto.'

'A cocktail party with crisps, peanuts, a glass of *vin ordinaire*, and a gold-plated watch. Thanks very much. But I'd rather have the full pension I'm entitled to.'

'And I want you to know, Arthur,' said Stratton, ignoring the outburst, 'how hard I fought your corner, but the board . . . well, I feel sure you know what they're like.'

Actually Arthur didn't have any idea what they were like. In fact if a member of the board had passed him in the street, he doubted if they would recognize him.

'But I did manage one small coup on your behalf,' continued Stratton, the same insincere smile returning to his face. 'I got you a stay of execution.' And from the look on the manager's face, he clearly regretted the words the moment he'd uttered them, but it didn't stop him charging on. 'While everyone else will have to leave by the end of the next quarter, six months at the most, you can retain your position as the senior VP for another year.'

'Just six months before I would have scraped over the line,' said Arthur with considerable feeling.

'I did the best I could given the circumstances,' insisted Stratton. 'And will be writing to you in the next few days, setting out the finer details.' The manager hesitated for a moment before adding, 'I was rather hoping, Arthur, I might rely on you to brief other senior colleagues of the board's decision. You're so good at that sort of thing.'

Arthur rose from his place with as much dignity as he could muster, and said calmly, 'Go to hell, Gerald. You can do your own dirty work for a change.' He gave the manager the same ingratiating smile, and left without another word.

Once Arthur was back in his office, he swore out loud, something he hadn't done since the Toronto Maple Leafs lost to the Montreal Canadiens during the last minute of extra time in the Stanley Cup.

He paced aimlessly around his little office for some time before he finally sat down and began to write a letter to Mr Macpherson explaining why someone else would be handling his account in the future.

★ ★ ★

A fortnight passed, but there was no reply from Ambrose Hall. This surprised Arthur, because if there was one thing he knew about his most esteemed customer, it was that he was never less than courteous and unfailingly punctilious.

The bank's senior VP continued to double-check his mail every morning, but there was still no response to his letter. Even more out of character, when quarter day appeared on the calendar, the usual long typewritten letter detailing Mr Macpherson's investment instructions and any other requirements he expected the bank to carry out during the next three months did not appear.

It was while Arthur was trying to get to sleep that the only other possibility for Mr Macpherson's uncharacteristic behaviour crossed Arthur's mind. He sat bolt upright and didn't sleep that night.

Nevertheless, it was still another fortnight before Arthur would accept that the 'only other possibility' had become a probability. But it wasn't until he'd opened a letter from Mr Stratton confirming the day of his retirement and his pension details, that the first dishonest thought crossed Arthur Dunbar's mind in twenty-eight years of service to the National Bank of Toronto.

However, Arthur was, by nature, a cautious man, so he allowed the dishonest thought to mature for a while before he even considered a provisional plan — and then only in his mind.

During the following month, he continued to clear every cheque that was presented in his client's name, as well as Mr and Mrs Laidlaw's monthly banker's order deposited to their joint account at the Bank of Scotland in Ambrose. However, when a new chequebook arrived from the printers, Arthur did not send it on to Mr Macpherson, but locked it in the top drawer of his desk.

He felt confident that would elicit an immediate response if . . .

Arthur kept rereading the letter that had landed on his desk. It was hand delivered by Mr Stratton's secretary, and was short and to the point.

It is with much regret . . .

Nowhere in the letter were the words 'sacked' or 'made redundant', because they had been replaced with wishing him a happy retirement, and how much he was looking forward to continuing working with him for the next ten months. Arthur swore for the second time that year.

The rest of the month passed without incident, although no letter was forthcoming from Mr Macpherson. The staff party was considered a great success by everyone except Arthur, who was the last to leave, and spent Christmas alone.

⋆   ⋆   ⋆

Arthur checked his calendar: 7 January, and he still hadn't received any further communication from Mr Macpherson, although he was aware any payments would soon come to an end, because he hadn't issued a new chequebook for the past quarter. But then Arthur was in no hurry, because he still had another nine months to work on his exit strategy, as befitted a banker who believed in the long game.

When no instructions came from Mr Macpherson by the end of the following quarter, Arthur decided he must either be too ill to communicate, or he was dead. He considered his next move most carefully. He thought about writing to Mr Macpherson concerning a recent dividend he'd received from the Shell Oil Company, asking if he wanted to accept payment, or to take up their offer of new shares. After considerable thought, he didn't send the letter, as he feared it might alert Mr and Mrs Laidlaw to the fact that someone at the bank was becoming suspicious.

Arthur decided he would wait for the cheques to run out before he made his next move, and every time a new chequebook arrived from the printers, he placed it in his top drawer along with the others.

Patience paid off, because the Laidlaws finally gave themselves away. When the last four cheques were sent to be cleared, Arthur noted that the sums were becoming larger and larger, and he made a bold decision that, despite the account still having over eight million dollars in cash, stocks and bonds, he would 'bounce' the final cheque made out to Cooks Travel for a package holiday for two in Ibiza. He waited for an irate letter from Mr Macpherson demanding an explanation, but none was forthcoming, which gave Arthur the confidence to put the second part of his plan into action.

2

Whenever anyone at the bank asked Arthur where he was going for his summer holiday, and not many people did, he always replied, 'I will be visiting my sister in Vancouver.' However, by the time it came for him to leave for his summer vacation, he not only had a sister, but a whole family in place: Eileen and Mike, who worked in local government, and a niece and nephew, Sue and Mike Jr. Not very imaginative, but when you haven't lied for twenty-nine years, your friends and colleagues have a tendency to accept everything you tell them.

During the next month, Arthur continued to invest Mr Macpherson's fortune in an orderly, if somewhat conservative fashion, keeping to a well-trodden path. At the same time, he withdrew small amounts of cash each week from his personal account, until he had a little over three thousand dollars locked away in his top drawer, not unlike a bridegroom preparing for his wedding.

On the Monday morning a week before he was due to go on holiday, Arthur placed the cash in his lunch box and headed off for his favourite bench in the park. However, on the way he dropped into the Royal Bank of Canada, where he waited in line at the currency counter, before changing his dollars into pounds.

During the Tuesday lunchbreak, he made a

181

further detour, to a local travel agent, where he purchased a return flight to Vancouver. He paid by cheque, and when he arrived back at the bank, left the ticket on the corner of his desk for all to see, and if anyone mentioned it, he once again told them all about his sister Eileen and her family in Vancouver.

On the Wednesday, Arthur applied for a new credit card on Mr Macpherson's behalf, and issued an order to cease any trading on the old one. A bright, shiny black card appeared on his desk forty-eight hours later. Arthur was ready to carry out stage two of his plan.

He had carefully chosen the dates he would be away from the office, selecting the two weeks before Mr Stratton was due to take his annual leave.

Arthur left the bank just after six on Friday evening, and took the usual bus back to his small apartment in Forest Hill. He spent a sleepless night wondering if he'd made the right decision. However, by the time the sun eventually rose on Saturday morning, he was resolved to go ahead with his plan and, as his father would have said, 'let the devil take the hindmost'.

After a leisurely breakfast, he packed a suitcase and left the flat just before midday. Arthur hailed a cab, an expense he normally wouldn't have considered, but then for the next few days everything he did would be out of character.

When the cab dropped him off at the domestic terminal, Arthur went straight to the Air Canada desk and traded in his return flight to Vancouver for a one-way window seat at the back of a plane

182

destined for London. He paid the difference in cash. Arthur then took the shuttle bus across to the international terminal, where he was among the first to check in. While he waited to board the aircraft, he sat behind a large pillar and, head down, remained hidden behind the *Toronto Star*. He intended to be among the first on, and the last off the plane, as he hoped it would cut down the chances of anyone recognizing him.

Once he'd fastened his seat belt, he made no attempt to strike up a conversation with the young couple seated next to him. During the seven-hour flight, he watched two films, which he wouldn't have bothered with back at home, and in between pretended to be asleep.

When the plane touched down at Heathrow the following morning, he waited patiently in line at Immigration, and by the time his passport had been stamped, his one suitcase was already circling around on the baggage carousel. Once he'd cleared Customs, he took another shuttle bus to terminal five, where he purchased a ticket to Edinburgh, which he also paid for in cash. On his arrival in the Scottish capital, another taxi took him to the Caledonian, a hotel recommended by the cabbie.

'How long will you be staying with us, sir?' asked the receptionist.

'Just the night,' replied Arthur, as she handed him his room key.

Arthur feared he'd have another restless night, but in fact fell asleep within moments of putting his head on the pillow.

The following morning, he ordered breakfast in bed, another first. But the moment he heard nine chiming on a nearby clock, he picked up the phone on his bedside table and dialled a number he did not have to look up.

'Royal Bank of Scotland, how can I help you?'

'I'd like to speak to the senior accounts manager,' said Arthur.

'Buchan,' said the next voice that came on the line. 'How can I help you?'

'I'm thinking of moving my account to your bank,' said Arthur, 'and wondered if I could make an appointment to see you as soon as possible.'

'Of course,' said the voice, suddenly sounding more obliging. 'Would eleven o'clock this morning suit you, Mr . . . ?'

'Macpherson,' said Arthur. 'Yes, that would be just fine.'

Arthur left the hotel just after ten thirty and, following the doorman's instructions, made his way down Princes Street, occasionally stopping to window shop, as he didn't want to be early for his appointment.

He entered the bank at 10.55 a.m., and a receptionist accompanied him to Mr Buchan's office. The senior accounts manager rose from behind his desk and the two men shook hands.

'How can I help you, Mr Macpherson?' Buchan asked once his potential new client had sat down.

'I'll be moving back to Scotland in a few

months' time,' said Arthur, 'and your bank was recommended to me by the senior vice president at NBT.'

'Our partner bank in Toronto,' said Buchan, as he opened a drawer in his desk and extracted some forms.

For the next twenty minutes, Arthur answered a series of questions that he was in the habit of asking. Once the last box had been filled in, and Arthur had signed *S. Macpherson* on the dotted line, Buchan asked if he had any form of identity with him, such as a passport.

'I'm so sorry,' said Arthur, 'I left my passport at the Caledonian. But I do have my credit card.'

The production of a platinum credit card seemed to be more than enough to satisfy the account manager.

'Thank you,' said Buchan, as he handed back the card. 'And may I ask when you expect the transfer to take place?'

'Sometime in the next few weeks,' replied Arthur, 'but I will ask Mr Dunbar, the bank's senior vice president, who has handled my account for the past twenty years, to give you a call.'

'Thank you,' said Buchan, making a note of the name. 'I look forward to hearing from him.'

Arthur walked slowly back to his hotel feeling the meeting couldn't have gone much better. He collected his case from his room, and returned to reception.

'I hope you enjoyed your stay with us, Mr Macpherson,' said the receptionist, 'and it won't be too long before we see you again.'

'In the not too distant future, I hope,' said Arthur, who settled his bill in cash, left the hotel, and asked the doorman to hail a taxi.

When he was dropped off at the station, Arthur joined another queue, and purchased a first-class return ticket to Ambrose. He sat alone in a comfortable carriage watching the country-side race by as the train travelled deeper and deeper into the Highlands, skirting several lochs and pine forests, which he might have enjoyed had he not been going over the most crucial part of his plan.

To date, everything had run smoothly, but Arthur had long ago accepted the real hurdle that still needed to be crossed would be when he came face to face with Mr and Mrs Laidlaw for the first time.

On arrival in Ambrose, Arthur climbed into the back of another taxi, and asked the driver to take him to the best hotel in town. This was greeted with a chuckle, followed by, 'You've obviously never visited these parts before. You have two choices, the Bell Inn or the Bell Inn.'

Arthur laughed. 'Well then, that's settled. And can I also book you for ten o'clock tomorrow morning?'

'Yes, sir,' said the driver cheerfully. 'Would you prefer this car, or I also have a limousine?'

'The limousine,' said Arthur, without hesitation. He needed the Laidlaws to realize who they were dealing with.

'And where will we be going?' the driver asked, as they drew up outside the Bell Inn.

'Ambrose Hall.'

The driver turned and gave his passenger a second look, but said nothing.

Arthur walked into the pub, where the bar doubled as the reception desk. He booked a room for the night, and told the landlord he couldn't be certain how long he would be staying, not adding, because if the front door of Ambrose Hall was opened by Mr Macpherson, he'd be on the next flight back to Toronto.

Once Arthur had unpacked, taken a bath and changed his clothes, he made his way back downstairs to the bar. The few locals stared at him disapprovingly, assuming he was an Englishman, until he opened his mouth, when their smiles returned.

He ordered cock-a-leekie soup and a Scotch egg, delighted to find that although the regulars continued to view him with suspicion, the landlord seemed quite happy to chat, especially if it was accompanied by the offer of a wee dram.

During the next hour and after nearly emptying a bottle of wee drams, Arthur discovered that no one in the town had ever met Mr Macpherson, although, the landlord added, 'the shopkeepers have no complaints, because the man always pays his bills on time and supports several local charities' — which Arthur could have listed. He noted the words 'pays' and 'supports', so certainly the landlord thought Macpherson was still alive.

'Came over from Canada in my father's day,' continued the barman. 'Said to have made a fortune on the railroad, but who knows the truth?'

187

Arthur knew the truth.

'Must be lonely up there in the winter,' said Arthur, still fishing.

'And the ice rarely melts on those hills before March,' said the barman. 'Still the old man's got the Laidlaws to take care of him, and she's a damned fine cook, even if he's not the most sociable of people, especially if you stray onto his land uninvited.'

'I think I'll turn in,' said Arthur.

'Care for a nightcap?' asked the landlord, holding up an unopened bottle of whisky.

'No, thank you,' said Arthur.

The landlord looked disappointed, but bade his guest goodnight.

Arthur didn't sleep well, and it wasn't just jet lag: after the barman's remarks he feared Macpherson might still be alive, in which case the whole trip would have been a complete waste of time and money. And worse, if Stratton got to hear about it . . .

★ ★ ★

When the sun rose the following morning, which Arthur noted was quite late in this part of the world, he took a bath, got dressed and went downstairs to enjoy a breakfast that would have been appreciated in a New York deli: porridge with brown sugar, kippers, toast, marmalade and steaming hot coffee. He then returned to his room and packed his small suitcase, still not certain where he would be spending the night.

He came back downstairs and, on being

188

handed his bill, discovered just how many wee drams the landlord had enjoyed. But this was not somewhere to hand over a credit card in the name of Mr S. Macpherson. That remained in his wallet. For now, its only purpose had been to prove his identity to Mr Buchan. Arthur settled the bill with cash, which brought an even bigger smile to the landlord's face.

When Arthur stepped out of the hotel just before ten o'clock, he was greeted with the sight of a gleaming black Daimler.

'Good morning,' he said, as he climbed into the back seat and sank down into the comfortable leather upholstery.

'Good morning, sir,' said the driver. 'Hope the car's to your liking.'

'Couldn't be better,' replied Arthur.

'Usually only comes out for weddings or funerals,' admitted the driver.

Arthur still wasn't sure which this was going to be.

The driver set off on the journey to Ambrose Hall, and it quickly became clear he hadn't visited the house for some time, and like everyone else in the town, had never set eyes on Mr Macpherson, but he added with a chuckle, 'They'll have to call for Jock when the old man dies.'

Once again Arthur feared his client must still be alive.

The hall turned out to be a journey of about fourteen miles, during which the roads became lanes, and the lanes, paths, until he finally saw a turreted castle standing four-square on a hill in the distance. Arthur had one speech prepared, should Mr Macpherson answer the door, and another if he was met by the Laidlaws.

The car proceeded slowly up the driveway, and they must have been about a hundred yards from the front door when Arthur first saw him. A massive giant of a man wearing a tartan kilt, with a cocked shotgun under his right arm, looking as if he hoped a stag might stray across his path.

'That's Hamish Laidlaw,' whispered Jock, 'and if you don't mind, I think I'll stay in the car.'

When Arthur got out, he heard the car doors lock. He began walking slowly towards his prey.

'What di ye want?' demanded Laidlaw, his gun rising a couple of inches.

'I've come to see Mr Macpherson,' said Arthur, as if he was expected.

'Mr Macpherson doesn't welcome strangers, especially those who dinnae have an appointment,' he said, the gun rising a couple more inches.

'He'll want to see me,' said Arthur, who took out his wallet, extracted a card, and handed it to the giant. Arthur suspected this might be one of those rare occasions when senior vice president embossed in gold below National Bank of Toronto might just have the desired effect.

While Laidlaw studied the card, Arthur watched as a moment of apprehension crossed his face, a look he'd experienced many times when a customer was asking for an overdraft, and didn't have the necessary security to back it up. The balance of power had shifted, and Arthur knew it.

'He's not here at the moment,' said Laidlaw, as the gun dropped.

'I know he isn't,' said Arthur, taking a risk,

'but if you don't want the whole town to know why I've come to visit you,' he added, looking back at Jock, 'I suggest we go inside.' He began walking slowly towards the front door.

Laidlaw got there just in time to open it, and led the intruder into the drawing room, where all the furniture was covered in dust sheets. Arthur pulled one off and let it fall to the floor. He sat down in a comfortable leather chair, looked up at Laidlaw and said firmly, 'Fetch Mrs Laidlaw. I need to speak to both of you.'

'She wasn't involved,' said Laidlaw, fear replacing bluster.

Involved in what? thought Arthur, but repeated, 'Fetch your wife. And while you're at it, Laidlaw, put that gun away, unless you want to add murder to your other crimes.'

Laidlaw scurried away, leaving Arthur to enjoy the magnificent paintings by Mackintosh, Farquharson and Peploe that hung on every wall. Laidlaw reappeared a few minutes later with a middle-aged woman in tow. She was wearing an apron, and didn't raise her head. It wasn't until she stopped half a pace behind her husband that Arthur realized just how much she was shaking.

'I know exactly what you two have been up to,' said Arthur, hoping they would believe him, 'and if you tell me the truth, and I mean the whole truth, there's just a chance I might still be able to save you. If you don't, my next visit will be to the local police station. I'll start with you, Mrs Laidlaw.'

'We didnae mean to do it,' she said, 'but he didn't leave us with a lot of choice.'

191

'Hold your tongue, woman,' said Laidlaw. 'I'll speak for both of us.'

'You'll do nothing of the sort,' said Arthur. He looked back at Mrs Laidlaw and played what he hoped was his trump card. 'The first thing I want to know is when Mr Macpherson died?'

'Just a few months back,' said Mrs Laidlaw. 'I found him in bed, white as a sheet he was, so he must have passed away during the night.'

'Then why didn't you call for a doctor, the police, even Jock?'

'Because we didn't think straight,' she said. 'We thought we'd lose our jobs and be turfed out of the lodge. So we waited to see what would happen if we did nothing, and as the monthly cheque kept arriving from the bank, we assumed no one could be any the wiser.'

'What did you do with the body?'

'We buried him. On the other side of the copse,' chipped in Mr Laidlaw, 'where no one would find him.'

'We didn't mean any harm,' she said, 'but we'd served the laird for over twenty years, and not so much as a pension.'

I know the feeling, thought Arthur, but didn't interrupt.

'We didn't steal nothing,' said Laidlaw.

'But you signed cheques in his name, and also went on receiving your monthly pay packet.'

'Only enough to keep us alive, and not allow the house to go to rack and ruin.'

'I told him we had to keep the expenses low,' said Mrs Laidlaw, 'so they wouldn't become suspicious.'

'That's what gave you away,' said Arthur.

'Will we go to jail?' asked Mrs Laidlaw.

'Not if you carry out my instructions to the letter,' said Arthur as he stood up. 'Is that understood?'

'I don't care about going to jail,' said Laidlaw, 'but not Morag. It wasn't her fault.'

'I'm afraid you're both in this together,' said Arthur.

Mrs Laidlaw began to shake again. 'Now I want to see Mr Macpherson's study.'

The Laidlaws both looked surprised by the request, but quickly led Arthur out of the drawing room and up a wide sweeping staircase to a large comfortable room on the first floor that had been converted to an office.

Arthur walked across to a desk that overlooked the hills of Arbroath. He was surprised to find not a speck of dust on the furniture, only perpetuating the myth that their master was still alive. The Laidlaws stood a few paces back, as their unwelcome visitor sat down at the desk. A flicker of a smile crossed Arthur's lips when he spotted the Remington Imperial typewriter on which Mr Macpherson had written so many letters to him over the years.

'Would you like a cup of tea, sir?' asked Mrs Laidlaw, as if she were addressing the master of the house.

'That would be nice, Morag,' said Arthur. 'Milk and one sugar, please.'

She disappeared, leaving her husband almost standing to attention. Arthur opened the top drawer of the desk to find a stack of used chequebooks, the stubs filled in with Macpherson's familiar neat hand. He closed the drawer and took out a piece of Ambrose Hall headed notepaper, and slipped it into the typewriter.

Arthur began to write a letter to himself, and after he'd typed 'Yours sincerely', he pulled the page out and read it, before turning to Laidlaw. 'I want you to read this letter carefully and then sign it.'

Laidlaw couldn't hide his surprise long before he finished reading the letter. But he took the quill pen from its holder, dipped it in the inkwell and slowly wrote 'S. Macpherson'. Arthur was impressed, and wondered how long it had taken Laidlaw to perfect the forgery, because he'd never spotted it. He took an envelope from the letter rack, placed it in the machine and typed:

Mr A. Dunbar
Senior Vice President
The National Bank of Toronto

He placed the letter in the envelope and sealed it, as Mrs Laidlaw returned carrying a tray of tea and shortbread biscuits. Arthur took a sip. Just perfect. He placed the cup back on its saucer and set about writing a second letter. When he had finished, he asked Laidlaw to once again add the false signature, but this time he didn't allow him to read the contents.

'Post one today,' said Arthur. 'And this one a week later,' he added, before passing both envelopes across to Laidlaw. 'If the second letter arrives on my desk within a fortnight, I shall return in a few weeks' time. If it doesn't your next visitor will be a police officer.'

'But how will we survive while you're away?' asked Laidlaw.

Arthur opened his briefcase and took out three chequebooks. 'Use them sparingly,' he said, 'because if I consider you have overstepped the mark, the cheque will not be cleared. Is that understood?' They both nodded. 'And you'll also need to order some more writing paper and envelopes,' continued Arthur, as he opened the drawer. 'And stamps.'

Arthur was just about to close the drawer when he spotted some documents tucked away in a corner. He pulled out Mr Macpherson's old passport, his birth certificate, and a will, and could feel his heart hammering in his chest. The three finds supplied him with a wealth of information that might prove useful in the future, and he finally discovered what the S. stood for. Macpherson's passport also revealed that he was sixteen years older than Arthur, but given the blurriness of the old photograph he felt he could get away with it. But he would still need to order a replacement before he returned to Toronto. He placed the passport, birth certificate and the will in his briefcase and locked it. He stood up and began to walk towards the door. The Laidlaws followed obediently in his wake.

'Mrs Laidlaw, I want all the dust sheets removed, and the house returned to the state it was in when Mr Macpherson was still in residence. Spare no expense, just be certain to send me every bill, so I can double-check it,' he added, as they walked downstairs together.

'By the time you return, Mr Dunbar, everything will be just as you would expect it,' she promised.

'As Mr Macpherson would expect it,' Arthur corrected her.

'Mr Macpherson,' she said. 'I'll prepare the master bedroom so it will be just like old times.'

'Is there anything else you'd like me to do, sir?' asked Laidlaw when Arthur reached the bottom of the staircase.

'Just be sure to post those two letters, and carry on as if Mr Macpherson was still alive, because he is,' said Arthur, as Laidlaw opened the front door.

When Jock saw them coming out of the house with Hamish Laidlaw clutching on to his hat, and no longer holding a gun, he jumped out of the car, ran around and opened the back door so his fare could climb in.

'Where to, sir?' said Jock.

'The station,' Arthur said, as he looked out of the window to acknowledge the Laidlaws waving, as if he were already the master of Ambrose Hall.

★   ★   ★

During the flight back to Heathrow, Arthur studied Mr Macpherson's last will and testament line by line. He had left generous legacies to the Laidlaws, while no other individual was mentioned. The bulk of the estate was to be divided between several local organizations and charities, the two largest amounts being allocated to the Scottish Widows and Orphans Fund, and the Rehabilitation of Young Offenders Trust. Did those simple bequests, Arthur wondered, explain why the young Scot had set sail for Canada, and ended his days as a recluse in a remote part of his homeland?

Arthur knew the passport and birth certificate could prove useful if he was to go ahead with the deception, but had already decided that when he died, the executors would find the will exactly where Mr Macpherson had left it.

On arrival back at Heathrow, Arthur took a train to Paddington and a taxi on to Petty France. Once he'd entered the building, he spent some considerable time filling in a long form, something he was rather good at.

After double-checking every box, he joined a slow-moving queue, and when he eventually reached the front he handed the document to a young lady seated behind the counter. She studied the application carefully, before asking to see Mr Macpherson's old passport, which Arthur handed over immediately. He'd made only one subtle change, 1950 had become 1966, while his own photograph had replaced the original one. She was clearly surprised not to have to make any corrections on his application form, or ask for further information. She smiled up at Arthur and stamped APPROVED.

'If you come back tomorrow afternoon, Mr Macpherson,' she said, 'you'll be able to pick up your new passport.'

Arthur thought about making a fuss as he had

a flight booked for Toronto that night, but simply said, 'Thank you,' as he didn't want to be remembered.

Arthur checked into a nearby hotel, where he spotted a poster advertising a performance of Schubert's Fifth, to be given at the Festival Hall by the Berlin Philharmonic under their conductor, Simon Rattle.

He was beginning to think the trip couldn't have gone much better.

3

Arthur picked up the phone on his desk and pressed a button that would put him through to the manager's office.

'Barbara, it's Arthur Dunbar.'

'Welcome back, Arthur. Did you have a nice time in Vancouver?'

'Couldn't have been better. In fact I'm considering moving out there when I retire.'

'We'll all miss you,' said Barbara. 'I'm not sure how the place will survive without you.'

'I'm sure it will,' said Arthur, 'but when are you expecting Mr Stratton back?'

'He and his wife flew to Miami on Friday. He'll be away for three weeks, so there couldn't be a better time for us to rob the bank.'

'And run away together,' laughed Arthur. 'Toronto's answer to Bonnie and Clyde! Still, while I'm the senior officer, could you keep me briefed if anything important arises?'

'Of course,' said Barbara. 'But as you well know, not a lot happens in August while so many customers are away on holiday. But I'll give you a buzz if anything comes up.'

* * *

Arthur checked his post every morning, but it wasn't until the sixth day that the first of the two letters landed on his desk. Arthur didn't rest on the seventh day, now he felt confident that the Laidlaws were keeping their side of the bargain. He picked up the phone and pressed another button.

'Standing orders,' said a voice he recognized.

'Steve, it's Arthur Dunbar. I've just received a letter from Mr Macpherson, and he's instructed the bank to raise Mr and Mrs Laidlaw's monthly allowance.'

'I wish someone would do that for me,' said Steve.

'I'll send down a copy of the letter for your files,' said Arthur, ignoring the comment. 'And can you make sure that everything is in place for the September payment.'

'Of course, Mr Dunbar.'

The second letter took a little longer to arrive, and Arthur even wondered if the Laidlaws had changed their mind, until the post boy delivered an envelope postmarked Ambrose on Monday morning, leaving him only five working days to complete the next part of his plan. But like a good Boy Scout, Arthur was well prepared.

He checked his watch. Buchan would still be at his desk for at least another couple of hours, but he needed to make an internal call before he contacted Edinburgh. He picked up the phone, pressed another button and waited until the head of accounts came on the line.

'Have you seen a copy of the Macpherson letter, Reg, that I sent down to your office earlier this morning?'

'Yes I have,' replied Caldercroft, 'and I'm sorry, Arthur, because you must be disappointed after all these years.'

'It was bound to happen at some time,' said Arthur.

'But sad that it's just when you're leaving. Will you get in touch with Mr Macpherson and try to persuade him to change his mind?'

'Not much point,' said Arthur. 'He hasn't done so for the past twenty years, so why would he now?'

'I'm sure you're right,' said Caldercroft. 'But shouldn't we wait until Stratton gets back, and see how he wants to play it?'

'I'm afraid the new banking laws don't allow us that luxury,' said Arthur. 'If a client requests to move his account, we must carry out their wishes within fourteen days, and as you can see, the letter is dated the eleventh.'

'Perhaps we should call Mr Stratton in Miami, and alert him to the situation?'

'You call him if you want to, Reg . . . '

'No, no,' said Caldercroft. 'You're in charge during the manager's absence, so what do you want me to do next?'

'Gather up all Mr Macpherson's bonds, stocks and any other financial instruments, and courier them to a Mr Buchan at RBS in Edinburgh, who appears to be the person he's appointed to take over the account. I'm just about to phone Buchan and find out when it will be convenient to complete the transfer. I'll keep you briefed.' He put the phone down.

Arthur took a deep breath and checked over his script one more time before he picked up the phone again and asked the switchboard operator to get him a number in Edinburgh. He waited to be put through.

'Good morning, Mr Buchan, my name is Arthur Dunbar, and I'm the senior VP at the National Bank of Toronto.'

'Good morning, Mr Dunbar,' said his opposite number. 'I've been expecting your call. I had a visit from a Mr Macpherson a couple of weeks ago, and he said you'd be in touch.'

'Indeed,' said Arthur, 'although we will be sorry to lose Mr Macpherson, a most valued client, but pleased he'll be moving to our partner bank in Edinburgh. And to that end,' said Arthur, trying to sound pompous, 'I have already given instructions to send all the necessary paperwork to you by courier, which I anticipate should be dealt with by the end of the week.'

'Thank you, said Buchan, 'and when will it be convenient for you to transfer Mr Macpherson's current account?'

'Would Thursday morning suit you? Around this time.'

'That should be fine. I'll make sure everything is in place to receive the funds on Thursday afternoon, and may I ask roughly how much we should be looking out for?'

'I can't be certain of the exact figure,' said Arthur, 'because I won't know the dollar-sterling exchange rate until that morning. But it will certainly be in excess of four million pounds.'

There was no response, and Arthur even wondered if they'd been cut off. 'Are you still there, Mr Buchan?'

'Yes, I am, Mr Dunbar,' Buchan eventually

managed. 'And I look forward to hearing from you again on Thursday.'

★ ★ ★

Mr Stratton returned from his holiday the following Monday, and had only been in his office for a few minutes before he called for the senior vice president.

'Why didn't you try and contact me in Miami?' were his first words as Arthur entered the room.

'As you can see,' said Arthur, placing his own typewritten letter on the desk, 'Mr Macpherson's instructions couldn't have been clearer, and as I have no way of contacting him other than by post, there wasn't a lot I could do.'

'You could have held things up, even flown to Scotland to see if you could get him to change his mind, which I would have approved.'

'That would have been pointless,' said Arthur, 'as he had already visited RBS in Edinburgh and instructed a Mr Buchan to carry out the transfer as expeditiously as possible.'

'Which I see you did last Thursday.'

'Yes,' said Arthur. 'We just managed to complete the transaction within the time stipulated by the new government regulations.' Stratton pursed his lips. 'However, a little coup I thought you would appreciate,' continued Arthur, enjoying himself, 'the Toronto end handled the exchange from dollars into pounds sterling, earning the bank some seventy-three thousand, one hundred and forty-one dollars.'

'A small compensation,' said Stratton begrudgingly.

'How kind of you to say so, Gerald.'

★   ★   ★

Arthur spent his last month making sure everything was in apple pie order, no more than his mother would have expected, so by the time Reg Caldercroft moved into his office and took over as the new senior vice president, Arthur had only one responsibility left: preparing a farewell speech for his retirement party.

'I think I can safely say,' said Mr Stratton, 'that few people have served this bank more conscientiously, and certainly none longer, than Arthur Dunbar. Twenty-nine years, in fact.'

'Twenty-nine years and seven months,' said Arthur with some feeling, and several of the longer-serving staff stifled a laugh.

'We're all going to miss you, Arthur.' The insincere smile returning to the manager's lips. 'And we wish you a long and happy retirement when you leave us to join your family in Vancouver.'

Loud 'Hear, hears' followed this statement.

'And on behalf of the bank,' continued Stratton, 'it's my pleasure to present you with a Rolex Oyster watch, and I hope whenever you look at it, you will be reminded of your time at the bank. Let's all raise a glass to our senior vice president, Arthur Dunbar.'

'To Arthur,' said over a hundred voices, as they raised their glasses in the air, which was quickly followed by cries of 'speech, speech!'

from the guests. They all fell silent when Arthur walked up to the front and took Stratton's place.

'I'd like to begin,' said Arthur, 'by thanking those people, and in particular Barbara, for organizing such a splendid party, and to all of you for this magnificent gift. And to you, Gerald,' he said, turning to face the manager, 'I must say it will be quite hard to forget who gave me the watch, when engraved on the back is the inscription, 'To Arthur, from all his colleagues at NBT'.' Everyone laughed and applauded as Arthur strapped the watch on his wrist. 'And if any of you should ever find yourself at a loose end in Vancouver, do please look me up.' He didn't add, but should you do so, you won't find me.

Arthur was touched by how warm the applause was when he rejoined the guests.

'We'll all miss you,' said Barbara.

Arthur smiled at the bank's biggest gem. 'And I'll miss you,' he admitted.

4

Arthur left the bank at six o'clock on quarter day. He took the bus back to his small apartment and packed up all his belongings before spending his last night in Toronto.

The following morning, after handing over the keys to his apartment to the janitor, he took a cab to the airport. He only made one stop on the journey, when he donated four packed suitcases of his past to a grateful volunteer worker at the local Red Cross shop.

After checking in at the domestic terminal, Arthur boarded the midday flight for Vancouver. On arrival on the west coast, he collected his only suitcase from the carousel, and took a shuttle bus across to the international terminal. He waited in line before purchasing a business-class ticket to London, which he paid for with the last of his Canadian dollars. By the time Arthur boarded the plane he was so exhausted he slept for almost the entire flight.

When he landed at Heathrow and had passed through Customs, he once again transferred to terminal five and purchased a ticket to Edinburgh, also with cash. Arthur checked the departure board, and although he had an hour to spare, he made his way slowly across to gate 43. He stopped at every lavatory en route, locked himself into a cubicle, ripped out one page of his Canadian passport, tore it into little pieces and flushed it down the toilet.

By the time Arthur reached the check-in desk, all he had left of his old passport was the cover. Mr Dunbar dropped it into the bottom of a waste bin outside McDonald's.

'Will all passengers . . . '

Mr Macpherson stepped onto the plane.

On arrival in Edinburgh, Arthur took a taxi to the Caledonian Hotel and checked in.

'Welcome back,' said the desk clerk, as he checked his credit card against the customer's reservation. He handed him a room key and said, 'You've been upgraded, Mr Macpherson.'

'Thank you,' said Arthur, who was shown up to a small suite on the sixth floor, to be greeted with a bottle of champagne in an ice bucket, and a handwritten note of welcome from the manager. He gave the bellboy a handsome tip.

Once he'd unpacked, he called Mr Buchan and made an appointment to see him later that afternoon. Following a light lunch in the brasserie, Arthur took a stroll along Princes Street and arrived outside the bank with a few minutes to spare.

'How nice to see you again, Mr Macpherson,' said Buchan, leaping up from behind his desk when Arthur entered the account manager's office.

'It's nice to see you too,' said Arthur, as the two men shook hands.

'Can I offer you a tea or coffee?' asked Buchan once his client was seated.

'No, thank you. I only wanted to check that my bank in Toronto had carried out the transfer, and there hadn't been any problems.'

'None that I'm aware of,' said Buchan. 'In fact, the transfer couldn't have gone more smoothly, thanks to Mr Dunbar, and I'm looking forward to representing you in the future. So can I ask, Mr Macpherson, is there anything you require at the moment?'

'A new credit card and some chequebooks.'

'Can I suggest our gold club card,' said Buchan, 'which has a daily credit limit of one thousand pounds, with no security checks, and I've already put in an order for some new chequebooks, which should be with us by Monday. Would you like me to forward them on to Ambrose Hall?'

'That won't be necessary,' said Arthur, 'as I intend to spend a few days in Edinburgh before I return to Ambrose. So perhaps I can drop in on Monday and pick them up.'

'Then I'll put a foot on the pedal and make sure they're ready for you to collect by then.'

'And my old NBT card?' asked Arthur.

'We'll cancel that when we hand over the new one on Monday. Do you have enough cash to see you through the weekend?'

'More than enough,' said Arthur.

★　★　★

Arthur left the bank and began walking back down Princes Street. What he hadn't told Buchan was that he intended to do some shopping before he headed for Ambrose, and even take in a concert or recital. In fact he dropped into four shops on his way back to the hotel, and purchased three suits, six silk shirts, two pairs of Church's shoes and an overcoat in the sale. Arthur had done more shopping in three hours than he'd previously managed in three years. As he continued down Princes Street, Arthur stopped to look at the painting in the window of Munro's, a Peploe of a bowl of fruit that he much admired. But he already had half a dozen of his own. In any case, he decided it might not be wise to enter the gallery where Mr Macpherson had purchased so many pictures in the past, so he continued on his way back to the hotel.

After a cold shower and a change of clothes, Arthur made his way down to the hotel dining room, where he enjoyed an Aberdeen Angus steak with all the trimmings, and a bottle of red wine he had read about in one of the colour supplements.

By the time he'd signed the bill — he nearly forgot his name — he was ready for a good night's sleep. He was passing Scott's Bar on his way to the lifts when he turned and saw her image in the mirror. She was sitting on a stool at the far end of the bar sipping a glass of champagne. Arthur continued on towards the lifts, and when one opened, he hesitated, turned around and began walking slowly back towards the bar. Could she really have been that attractive? There was only one way he was going to find out. In any case, someone had probably joined her by now.

A second look, and he was even more

captivated. She must have been about forty, and the elegant green dress that rested just above her knees only convinced Arthur she couldn't possibly be alone. He strolled up to the bar and took a seat on a stool two places away from her. He ordered a drink, but he didn't have the nerve to even glance in her direction, and certainly wouldn't have considered striking up a conversation.

'Are you here for the conference?' she asked.

Arthur swung round and stared into those green eyes before murmuring, 'What conference?'

'The garden centres annual conference.'

'No,' said Arthur. 'I'm on holiday. But is that why you're here?'

'Yes, I run a small garden centre in Durham. Are you a gardener by any chance?'

Arthur thought about his flat in Toronto where he'd had a window box, and Ambrose Hall, that couldn't have been less than a thousand acres.

'No,' he managed. 'Always lived in a city,' he added, as she drained her champagne. 'Can I get you another?'

'Thank you,' she said, allowing the barman to refill her glass. 'My name's Marianne.'

'I'm Sandy,' he said.

'And what do you do, Sandy?'

'I dabble in stocks and shares,' he replied, taking on the persona of Macpherson. 'And when you said 'run', does that mean you're the boss?'

'I wish,' she said, and by the time Marianne's glass had been refilled three times, he'd discovered she was divorced, her husband had run away with a woman half his age, no children, and she had planned to go to the Schubert concert at the Usher Hall that night only to find it was sold out. After another drink, he even found out she didn't consider Brahms to be in the same class as Beethoven. He was already wondering how far the journey was from Edinburgh to Durham.

'Would you like another drink?' he asked.

'No, thank you,' she replied. 'I ought to be getting to bed if I'm still hoping to make the opening session tomorrow morning.'

'Why don't we go up to my suite? I have a bottle of champagne, and no one to share it with.' Arthur couldn't believe what he'd just said, and assumed she'd get up and leave without another word, and might even slap his face. He was just about to apologize, when Marianne said, 'That sounds fun.' She slipped off her stool, took his hand and said, 'Which floor are you on, Sandy?'

In the past, Arthur had only dreamed of such a night, or read about it in novels by Harold Robbins. After they'd made love a third time, she said, 'I ought to be getting back to my room, Sandy, if I'm not going to fall asleep during the president's address.'

'When does the conference end?' asked Arthur, as he sat up and watched her getting dressed.

'Usually around four.'

'Why don't I try to get a couple of tickets for the Schubert concert, and then we could have dinner afterwards.'

'What a lovely idea,' said Marianne. 'Shall we meet in reception at seven tomorrow evening?' She giggled. 'This evening,' she added, as she bent down and kissed him.

'See you then,' he said, and by the time the door had closed, Arthur had fallen into a deep contented sleep.

★ ★ ★

When Arthur woke the following morning, he couldn't stop thinking about Marianne, and decided to buy her a present and give it to her at dinner that evening. But first he must get two tickets, the best in the house for a show that was obviously sold out, and then ask the desk clerk which he considered was the finest restaurant in Edinburgh.

Arthur had a long shower, and found himself humming the aria from Mendelssohn's *Midsummer Night's Dream*. He continued to hum as he put on a new shirt, new suit and began to think about what sort of present Marianne would appreciate. Mustn't be over the top, but shouldn't leave her in any doubt he considered last night so much more than a one-night stand.

He went to his bedside table to pick up his wallet and watch, but they weren't there. He opened the drawer, and stared at a copy of Gideon's Bible. He quickly checked the table on the other side of the bed, and then the bathroom, and finally his new suit that was strewn on the floor. He sat on the end of the bed for some time, unwilling to accept the truth. He didn't want to believe such a divine creature could be a common thief.

He reluctantly picked up the phone by the side of the bed and dialled Mr Buchan's private number at the Royal Bank of Scotland. He sat there in a daze until he heard a voice he recognized on the other end of the line.

'I'm sorry to bother you,' said Arthur, 'but I've lost my credit card.'

'That's not a problem,' said Buchan. 'Happens all the time. I'll cancel it immediately and your new one will be ready for collection on Monday morning. If you need some cash in the meantime, just pop in and I'll arrange it.'

'No, I've got enough to get me through until Monday,' said Arthur, not wanting to admit that his money had also been stolen.

Arthur went downstairs for breakfast, and wasn't surprised to discover that there was no garden centres conference, and no one called Marianne registered at the hotel. When he left the Caledonian to go for a walk after breakfast, it was back to window shopping and he even spotted the ideal present for Marianne. It didn't help. And when he passed the Usher Hall on the way back, there was already a queue for returns. At least that was true.

It was a long weekend of walks around the ancient city, hotel food and watching B movies in his room that he'd already seen. When he walked past Scott's Bar on Saturday night and saw an attractive young blonde sitting alone, he just kept on walking.

By Monday he'd exhausted the hotel menu as

well as the films of the week and just wanted to return to Ambrose Hall and begin his new life. The only surprise was that he still couldn't get Marianne out of his mind.

5

By the time Arthur had packed his bags on Monday morning, he'd decided the loss of a couple of hundred pounds and a watch he'd never cared for, was a fair exchange for the best night he'd ever had in his life.

He checked his watch. It wasn't there. Arthur smiled for the first time in days. Once he'd seen Buchan, he would take the first train to Ambrose and try to forget the whole incident, but he knew he wouldn't be able to. He was feeling a little better by the time he left the hotel to keep his appointment with Mr Buchan, and when he walked into the bank, his secretary was standing in the hall waiting to greet him. A gesture, he realized, that was only extended to the most important customers.

'I hope you had an enjoyable weekend, Mr Macpherson?' she said, as she accompanied Arthur through to Mr Buchan's office.

'Yes, thank you,' he replied politely, as she opened the door and stepped aside to allow him to enter.

Arthur froze on the spot when he saw Mr Stratton seated on the right of Mr Buchan, with a large burly man he didn't recognize seated on his left.

'Sit down, Dunbar,' said Stratton, as the door closed behind him.

Arthur obeyed the manager's order as if they

were back in Toronto, but said nothing.

'It wasn't difficult for me to work out what you've been up to for the past year,' said Stratton, 'and at least we caught up with you before you could do any real damage. We have Chief Inspector Mullins of the Edinburgh city police to thank for that,' he added, revealing who the third person was.

Arthur still didn't speak, although he would have liked to ask the policeman how long his sentence was likely to be, but satisfied himself with, 'How did you find out?'

'The watch,' said Chief Inspector Mullins matter-of-factly. ' "To Arthur, from all his colleagues at NBT". Once we'd cracked NBT, the rest was easy. And after she'd described you as a nice gentleman with a mid-Atlantic accent, one call to the bank and Mr Stratton even told us he'd presented you with the Rolex Oyster.'

'And Marianne, how did you catch her?'

'She tried to buy a train ticket to Durham with your credit card, but fortunately Mr Buchan had already cancelled it.'

'And as far as I can tell,' said Stratton, taking over, 'you've only spent two thousand, seven hundred and eighty-two dollars of Mr Macpherson's money. However, that doesn't include the seventy-three thousand, one hundred and forty-one dollars the bank will have to return to Mr Macpherson's private account, following the abortive exchange rate deal.'

'And a further forty-nine thousand, one hundred and twenty-four pounds,' said Buchan, 'that will have to be charged to NBT after converting the four million pounds back into dollars.'

'Mr Buchan has already supplied me with all the share certificates, bonds and other financial instruments which I will be taking back to Toronto later today, and once I return, Mr Macpherson's account will be repaid in full. So with a bit of luck, he will never find out what happened. However,' Stratton continued, 'you have cost the National Bank of Toronto one hundred and twenty-three thousand, four hundred and sixty-eight dollars, not to mention the irreparable damage you might have caused to the bank's reputation had this story ever got out. But, thanks to the cooperation of the Edinburgh police, to whom we will be eternally grateful,' continued Stratton, nodding in the chief inspector's direction, 'if you will agree to cover any costs, they will not press charges.'

'And if I don't?' said Arthur.

'As a senior banking officer, in a position of trust,' said Chief Inspector Mullins, 'you could be looking at six to eight years in a Scottish prison. I would'nae recommend it, laddie,' he paused, 'given the choice.'

Mr Stratton stood up and walked down from the other end of the table and handed over a cheque made out to the bank for $123,468. All it needed was a signature.

'But that would almost clean me out.'

'Perhaps you should have thought about that in the first place,' said Stratton, handing him a pen.

Arthur reluctantly signed the cheque, accepting that the alternative, as Mullins had so subtly pointed out, wasn't that attractive.

Stratton retrieved the cheque and placed it in his wallet. He then turned to the chief inspector and said, 'Like you, we will not be pressing charges.'

Mullins looked disappointed.

Typical Stratton, thought Arthur. Make sure you cover your own backside, and to hell with everyone else. Arthur even wondered if the board would ever be told what had really happened. But Stratton hadn't finished. He picked up a carrier bag from under his chair, and emptied a pile of Canadian dollars onto the table in front of Arthur.

'Your account has been closed,' he said, 'and the bank is no longer willing to do business with you in the future.'

Arthur slowly gathered up the neat cellophane packages, aware that he would even be paying for Stratton's first-class flight back to Toronto. He dropped the money into the carrier bag.

'And what about my watch, Chief Inspector?' said Arthur, turning to face Mullins.

'Mrs Dawson comes up in front of the magistrate at ten o'clock tomorrow morning, so you can collect it any time after that, but not until she's been sentenced.' He smiled at Arthur for the first time.

'I don't suppose you'd be willing to appear as a witness for the Crown?' he said, raising an eyebrow.

Arthur smiled back. 'You suppose correctly, Chief Inspector. I wouldn't, even if you'd made it a condition.'

Mullins frowned as Arthur rose from his place, and quietly left the room; no smiles, no handshakes, and certainly no one accompanied him to the front door. He left the bank in a daze and began to make his way slowly back to the hotel, not certain what to do next.

He'd only gone about a hundred yards along Princes Street, when he spotted a sign on a window in neat black letters, Henderson & Henderson, Attorneys at Law.

6

When the defendant took her place in the dock, she looked tired and vulnerable.

A court officer rose and read out the charges. 'Marianne Dawson, you come before the court on three charges. One: that you stole a credit card from a Mr Macpherson, and attempted to use it to purchase a rail ticket to Durham. How do you plead to this charge, guilty or not guilty?'

'Guilty,' said the defendant, almost in a whisper.

'The second charge,' continued the officer, 'is that you did steal a sum of around two hundred pounds from the said Mr Macpherson. How do you plead, guilty or not guilty?'

'Guilty,' she repeated.

'And the third count is that you did steal a Rolex Oyster watch also from the same gentleman. How do you plead, guilty or not guilty?'

Marianne looked up and facing the magistrate said quietly, 'Guilty.'

The chairman of the magistrates stared down into the well of the court and asked, 'Is the defendant represented?'

A tall, distinguished-looking man, dressed in a pinstriped suit, white shirt and black tie, rose from the bench and said, 'I have the privilege of representing Mrs Dawson.'

The Justice of the Peace was surprised to find

one of Edinburgh's leading advocates appearing before him on such a minor case.

'Mr Henderson, as your client has pleaded guilty to all three charges, I presume you will be offering a plea in mitigation?'

'I most certainly will, sir,' he said, tugging the lapels of his jacket. 'I would like to start by bringing to the attention of the court that Mrs Dawson has recently experienced a most acrimonious divorce, and despite the family division awarding her maintenance payments, her husband has made no attempt to fulfil his responsibility, even after a court order was issued against him. Until recently,' continued Mr Henderson, 'Mrs Dawson held a senior management position at the Durham Garden Centre, until it was taken over by Scotsdales, and she was made redundant. I feel sure the Bench will also take into consideration that this is a first offence, other than a parking fine some four years ago. However, Mrs Dawson is not only extremely remorseful, but determined to pay Mr Macpherson back every penny she owes him, just as soon as she can find a job. I would finally like to point out that until today, Mrs Dawson enjoyed an unblemished reputation as an upright citizen, which I hope the Bench will take into consideration before passing sentence.'

'I am grateful to you, Mr Henderson,' said the justice. 'Please allow me a few moments to consult with my colleagues.'

Henderson bowed, as the chairman and his two colleagues discussed the case among themselves, before coming to an agreement.

The chairman turned back to face the defendant.

'Mrs Dawson,' he began, 'despite learned counsel's moving plea in mitigation, someone in your position must have been well aware they were breaking the law.' Marianne bowed her head. 'So I am left with no choice but to sentence you to six months in prison, which will be suspended for two years. However, should you appear before me again, I will not hesitate to issue you with a custodial sentence. But on this occasion, I shall order you to pay a fine of two hundred pounds.' He switched his attention back to Mr Henderson, and asked, 'Is the defendant able to pay this sum?'

Mr Henderson turned round and looked towards the back of the courtroom where his client was seated. Arthur nodded.

7

Arthur took a piece of headed paper from the letter rack on his desk and placed it in the typewriter.

Dear Mr Stratton,

Thank you for your most recent letter, and the three new chequebooks that arrived this morning.

May I begin by placing on record how much I appreciate the years of dedicated service Mr Arthur Dunbar carried out on my behalf, and would you be kind enough to pass on my best wishes to him and the hope he will have a long and happy retirement.

I have checked my latest accounts which appear to be in order. However, I will be writing to you at the end of the quarter concerning some future investments I am presently considering.

I should also like you to know that I have recently married, so you may find a new pattern will emerge in some of my transactions. My wife and I intend to travel abroad occasionally, to visit the great concert halls and opera houses of Europe. While we're away, Mr and Mrs Laidlaw will continue to run Ambrose Hall, so you can expect the usual bills for household expenses in addition to their monthly salaries.

May I also add . . .

There was a knock at the door, and Arthur stopped typing. 'Come in.'

Morag popped her head round the door and said, 'I just wondered what you and Mrs Macpherson would like for lunch? I still have some of that game pie you're rather partial to.'

'Perfect,' said Arthur, 'but not too much. Mrs Macpherson has already chastised me for putting on weight.'

'And Mrs Macpherson also asked me to remind you that you're going into Edinburgh this evening for some concert.'

'Not some concert, Morag, Beethoven's Third at the Usher Hall.'

'Will there be anything else, sir?'

'Yes, I'm just finishing off a letter to Mr Stratton, so could you ask Hamish to come up? I'd like him to drive into the village and post it.'

'Of course, sir.'

Arthur returned to the letter.

May I also add how delighted I was to learn that you will personally be supervising my account in the future. It gives me succour to know that my affairs will be in such safe hands.

Yours sincerely

There was a knock on the door and Laidlaw walked in.

'You asked to see me, sir?'

'Yes, Hamish. Just a signature.'

A GOOD TOSS TO LOSE

Mr Gruber handed back the boys' essays before returning to his desk at the front of the class.

'Not a bad effort,' the young schoolmaster said, 'except for Jackson, who clearly doesn't believe Goethe is worthy of his attention. And as this is a voluntary class, I'm bound to ask, Jackson, why you bothered to enrol?'

'It was my father's idea,' admitted Jackson. 'He thought there might come a time when it would be useful to speak a little German.'

'How little did he have in mind?' asked the schoolmaster.

Jackson's friend Brooke, who was seated at the desk next to him, whispered loudly enough for everyone in the class to hear, 'Why don't you tell him the truth, Oliver?'

'The truth?' repeated Gruber.

'My father is convinced, sir, that it won't be too long before we are at war with Germany.'

'And why should he think that, may I ask? When Europe has never been at peace for such a long period of time.'

'I accept that, sir, but Pa works at the Foreign Office. Says the Kaiser is a warmonger, and given the slightest opportunity will invade Belgium.'

'But, remembering your treaty obligations,' said Gruber as he walked between the desks, 'that would also drag Britain and France into the conflict.' The schoolmaster paused for thought. 'So the real reason you want to learn German,' he continued, attempting to lighten the exchange, 'is so you can have a chat with the Kaiser when he comes marching down Whitehall.'

'No, I don't believe that's what Pa had in mind, sir. I think he felt that once the Kaiser had been sent packing, if I could speak a little German, I might be in line to be a regional governor.'

The whole class burst out laughing, and began to applaud.

'We must hope for the sake of your countrymen as well as mine, Jackson, that it's a very long line.'

'If Kaiser Bill were to wage war, sir,' said Brooke, sounding more serious, 'would you have to return to your country?'

'I pray that will never happen, Brooke,' said Gruber. 'I look upon England as my second home. Europe is at peace at the moment, so we must hope Jackson's father is wrong. Nothing would be gained from such a pointless act of folly other than to set the world back a hundred years. Let us be thankful that King George V and Kaiser Wilhelm are cousins.'

'I've never cared much for my cousin,' said Jackson.

★ ★ ★

'Have you heard the news?' said Brooke, as he and Jackson strolled across to the refectory a few weeks later.

'What news?' said Jackson.

'Mr Gruber will be returning to Germany within a fortnight.'

'Why?' said Jackson.

'It seems the headmaster thought it wise given the circumstances.'

'I'm sorry to hear that,' said Jackson as they sat down on a wooden bench and waited to be served lunch.

'But I thought you didn't like having to study German,' said Brooke, as he attempted to spear a soggy carrot with his fork.

'And I still don't. But that doesn't mean I don't like Mr Gruber. In fact he's always struck me as a thoroughly decent fellow. Not at all the sort of chap one would want to go to war with.'

'We might even be at war with him in a few months' time,' said Brooke, 'and if you're still thinking of making the army your career, you could find yourself on the front line.'

'I don't think you'll be exempt from that privilege, Rupert,' said Oliver, swamping his food with gravy, 'just because you're going up to Cambridge to swan around writing poetry.'

'Which reminds me,' said Brooke. 'My mother wondered if you'd like to join us in Grantchester for a couple of weeks this summer. And I can promise you some rather interesting gals will be joining us.'

'Can't think of anything better, old chap. That's assuming Kaiser Bill hasn't got other plans for us.'

★　★　★

Oliver Jackson did spend a couple of carefree weeks with his friend, Rupert Brooke, that summer, before they parted and went their separate ways. Brooke to read Classics at King's, while Jackson reported to the Royal Military Academy at Sandhurst, to accept the king's shilling and spend the next two years being trained as an officer in the British Army.

★　★　★

In October 1913, Second Lieutenant Jackson of the Lancashire Fusiliers reported to his regiment's depot in Chester, where he quickly discovered that talk of war with Germany was no longer confined to the Foreign Office, but was now on everyone's lips. However, no one could be sure what would light the fuse.

When Kaiser Wilhelm's close friend and ally, the Archduke Franz Ferdinand of Austria, was assassinated in Sarajevo, the German emperor had at last found the excuse he needed for his troops to invade Belgium, giving him the chance to expand his empire.

The only good thing that had happened while Oliver was serving his tour of duty in Chester was that he fell in love with a Miss Rosemary Carter, the daughter of one of his father's colleagues at the Foreign Office. In the fathers' eyes, the marriage was no more than an *entente cordiale*, whereas both mothers quickly realized that this particular treaty had never required Foreign Office approval.

One of the many things Kaiser Bill did to

irritate Oliver was to declare war while he and Rosemary were still on their honeymoon. Lieutenant Jackson received a telegram delivered to his Deauville hotel ordering him to report back to his regiment immediately.

★ ★ ★

A few weeks later the Lancashire Fusiliers were among the first to be shipped out to France, where Oliver quickly discovered that it was possible to live in far worse conditions and force down even more disgusting grub than he'd been made to endure at Rugby.

He settled down in a trench where rats were his constant companions, three inches of muddy water his pillow, and slowly learnt to sleep despite the sound of gunfire.

'It will be over by Christmas,' was the optimistic cry being passed down the line.

'But which Christmas?' asked a bus driver from Romford as he forked a billycan of corned beef and baked beans, while refilling his mug with rainwater.

In fact the only present the young subaltern got that Christmas was a third pip to be sewn next to the other two already on his shoulder, and then only after he replaced a brother officer who had not made it into 1915.

Captain Jackson had already been over the top three times by the winter of 1916, and didn't need reminding that the average survival period for a soldier on the front line was nineteen days; he was now in his third year. But at least they were allowing him to return home for a three-week furlough. What old soldiers referred to as a 'stay of execution'.

Jackson returned to the Marne after spending an idyllic carefree break with Rosemary in their country cottage at Crathorne. He was grateful to find that even his father was beginning to believe the war couldn't last much longer. Oliver prayed that he was right.

On arriving back at the front, Jackson immediately reported to his commanding officer.

'We are expecting to mount another attack on Jerry in a few days' time,' said Colonel Harding. 'So be sure your men are prepared.'

Prepared for what?, thought Oliver. Almost certain death, and not quick like the hangman's noose, but probably prolonged, in desperate agony. But he didn't voice his opinion.

Once he was back in the trenches, Oliver quickly tried to get to know the young impressionable men who'd just arrived at the front line, and hadn't yet heard a shot fired in anger. He couldn't think of them as soldiers, just keen young lads who had responded to a poster of a moustachioed old man pointing a finger at them and declaring YOUR COUNTRY NEEDS YOU.

'Once you go over the top, you need only remember one thing,' Oliver instructed them. 'If you don't kill them, as sure as hell they'll kill you. Think of it like a football match against your most bitter rivals. You've got to score every time you shoot.'

'But whose side is the ref on?' demanded a young, frightened voice.

Oliver didn't reply, because he no longer believed God was the referee and that therefore they must surely win.

★ ★ ★

The colonel joined them just before the kick-off and blew a whistle to show the match could begin. Captain Jackson was first over the top, leading his company, who followed closely behind. On, on, on, he charged as his men fell like fairground soldiers beside him, the lucky ones dying quickly. He kept going, and was beginning to wonder if he was out there on his own, and then suddenly, without warning, he saw a lone figure running through the whirling smoke towards him. Like Oliver, the man had his bayonet fixed, ready for the kill. Oliver accepted that it would not be possible for both of them to survive, and probably neither would. He held his rifle steady, like a medieval jouster, determined to fell his opponent. He was prepared to thrust his bayonet, not this time into a horsehair bag while training, but into a petrified human being, but no more petrified than he was.

Don't strike until you see can the whites of his eyes, his training sergeant had drilled into him at Sandhurst. You can't be a moment too early, or a moment too late. Another oft-repeated maxim. But when he saw the whites of his eyes, he couldn't do it. He lowered his rifle, expecting to die, but to his surprise the German also dropped his rifle as they both came to a halt in the middle of no-man's-land.

For some time they just stared at each other in disbelief. But it was Oliver who burst out laughing, if only to release his pent-up tension.

'What are you doing here, Jackson?'

'I might ask you the same question, sir.'

'Carrying out someone else's orders,' said Gruber.

'Me too.'

'But you're a professional soldier.'

'Death doesn't discriminate in these matters,' said Oliver. 'I often recall your shrewd opinion of war, sir, and looking around the battlefield can only wonder how much talent has been squandered here.'

'On both sides,' said Gruber. 'But it gives me no pleasure to have been proved right.'

'So what shall we do now, sir? We can't just stand around philosophizing until peace is declared.'

'But equally, if we were to return meekly to our own side, we would probably be arrested, court-martialled and shot at dawn.'

'Then one of us will have to take the other prisoner,' said Jackson, 'and return in triumph.'

'Not a bad idea. But how shall we decide?' asked Gruber.

'The toss of a coin?'

'How very British,' declared Gruber. 'Just a pity the whole war couldn't have been decided that way,' added the schoolmaster as he took a Goldmark out of his pocket. 'You call, Jackson,' he said. 'After all, you're the visiting team.'

Oliver watched as the coin spun high into the air and cried, 'Tails,' only because he couldn't bear the thought of the Kaiser's image staring up at him in triumph.

Gruber groaned as he bent down to look at the eagle. Oliver quickly took off his tie, bound the prisoner's wrists behind his back, and then began to march his old schoolmaster slowly back towards his own front line.

'What happened to Brooke?' asked Gruber as they squelched through the mud while stepping over the bodies of fallen men.

'He was attached to the Royal Naval Division when he last wrote to me.'

'I read his poem about Grantchester. Even attempted to translate it.'

' 'The Old Vicarage',' said Jackson.

'That's the one. Ironic that he wrote it while he was on a visit to Berlin. Such a rare talent. Let's hope he survives this dreadful war,' Gruber said as the sun dipped below the horizon.

'Are you married, sir?' asked Oliver.

'Yes. Renate. And we have a son and two daughters. And you?'

'Rosemary. Just got married when the balloon went up.'

'Bad luck, old chap,' said Gruber, before taking his former pupil by surprise. 'I don't suppose you'd consider being a godfather to my youngest, Hans? You see, I consider it no more than my duty once the war is over to make sure this madness can never happen again.'

'I agree with you, Ernst, and I'd be honoured. And perhaps in time . . . '

'May I suggest, Oliver, for both our sakes,' said Gruber as the British front line came into sight, 'that when you hand me over, you don't make it too obvious we're old friends.'

'Good thinking, Ernst,' said Oliver, and grabbed his prisoner roughly by the elbow.

The next voice they heard demanded, 'Who goes there?'

'Captain Jackson, Lancashire Fusiliers, with a German prisoner.'

'Advance and be recognized.' Oliver pushed his old schoolmaster forward. 'Bloody good show,' said the lookout sergeant. 'You can leave him to me, sir. And you can keep moving, you fucking Kraut.'

'Sergeant,' said Oliver sharply, 'try to remember he's an officer.'

★ ★ ★

The war was over by Christmas. Christmas 1918.

Captain Ernst Gruber spent two years in a prisoner-of-war camp on Anglesey. He passed the mornings teaching his fellow prisoners the local tongue as there might come a time when it would prove useful to speak a little English, he suggested, echoing Jackson's words.

Oliver sent Gruber the collected works of Rupert Brooke, which he translated in the evenings while he waited for the war to end.

Ernst Gruber was shipped back to Frankfurt in November 1919, and within days he wrote to Oliver to ask if he was still willing to be a godfather to his son Hans. It was several weeks before he received a reply from Oliver's wife

Rosemary, to say that her husband had been killed on the Western Front only days before the Armistice was signed. They also had a son, Arthur Oliver, and on her husband's last furlough he'd told her that he hoped Ernst would agree to be one of Arthur's godparents.

With the assistance of Oliver's father, Herr Gruber was allowed to visit England to fulfil his role in the christening ceremony. As Ernst stood by the font alongside Oliver's family, he couldn't help wondering what would have happened if he had won the toss.

Postscript

19 September 1943
LIEUTENANT HANS OTTO GRUBER was blown up by a landmine while serving on the Western Front. He died three days later.

6 June 1944
CAPTAIN ARTHUR OLIVER JACKSON MC was killed while leading his platoon on the beaches of Normandy.

15 November 1944
PROFESSOR ERNST HELMUT GRUBER was executed by firing squad in Berlin for the role he played in the failed attempt to assassinate Adolf Hitler at Wolf's Lair.

May They Rest in Peace

THE PERFECT MURDER

Coincidences are frowned upon in a novel, whereas in real life they regularly occur.

I had already read the proofs of *Tell Tale*, and returned them to my publisher, when *Reader's Digest* announced they would be relaunching their 100-word short story competition later this year.

The commissioning editor of *Reader's Digest* invited me to take up the challenge a second time, and produce a 100-word tale within twenty-four hours.

Result? 'The Perfect Murder'. I hope you enjoy my latest effort, and if you are a closet author yourself, perhaps you should finally come out, and also take up the challenge.

This is also a hundred words.

Albert stared at the prisoner standing in the dock, well aware he hadn't committed the murder.

Albert had struck the fatal blow moments after Yvonne admitted she was seeing another man. He slipped out of her flat and into a telephone box on the other side of the road. When his rival appeared, he dialled 999.

Twenty minutes later two detectives dragged the innocent man out of her apartment, threw him into the back of a police car and, sirens blazing, sped off.

'Do you find the defendant guilty or not guilty of murder?'

The foreman rose.

'Guilty,' said Albert.

We do hope that you have enjoyed reading this large print book.

Did you know that all of our titles are available for purchase?

We publish a wide range of high quality large print books including:
Romances, Mysteries, Classics
General Fiction
Non Fiction and Westerns

Special interest titles available in large print are:
The Little Oxford Dictionary
Music Book
Song Book
Hymn Book
Service Book

Also available from us courtesy of Oxford University Press:
Young Readers' Dictionary
(large print edition)
Young Readers' Thesaurus
(large print edition)

For further information or a free brochure, please contact us at:
Ulverscroft Large Print Books Ltd.,
The Green, Bradgate Road, Anstey,
Leicester, LE7 7FU, England.
Tel: (00 44) 0116 236 4325
Fax: (00 44) 0116 234 0205

THIS WAS A MAN

Jeffrey Archer

The conclusion to the Clifton Chronicles. Giles Barrington discovers the truth about his wife Karin from the cabinet secretary. Is she a spy, or a pawn in a larger game? Harry Clifton sets out to write his magnum opus, while his wife Emma completes her ten years as chairman of the Bristol Royal Infirmary, and receives an unexpected call from Margaret Thatcher offering her a job. Sebastian Clifton becomes chairman of Farthings Kaufman bank after Hakim Bishara resigns for personal reasons. Sebastian and his wife Samantha's talented daughter Jessica is expelled from the Slade School of Art. Lady Virginia is about to flee the country to avoid her creditors when the Duchess of Hertford dies, and she sees an opportunity to finally trump the Cliftons and the Barringtons. Then tragedy engulfs the Clifton family . . .

COMETH THE HOUR

Jeffrey Archer

Giles Barrington must decide if he should withdraw from politics and try to rescue Karin, the woman he loves, from behind the Iron Curtain. But is Karin truly in love with him, or is she a spy? Meanwhile, Lady Virginia is facing bankruptcy, and can see no way out of her financial problems — until she is introduced to the hapless Cyrus T. Grant III . . . Sebastian Clifton is now chief executive of Farthings Bank, and a workaholic; his personal life is thrown into disarray when he falls for Priya, a beautiful Indian girl. But her parents have already chosen the man she is going to marry . . . And Sebastian's rivals, Adrian Sloane and Desmond Mellor, are still plotting against him and his chairman, Hakim Bishara, so they can take over Farthings . . .